WORLD SPLIT OPEN

WORLD SPLIT OPEN

Elisabeth Klein

REDEMPTION PRESS

World Split Open
© 2014 by Elisabeth Klein. All rights reserved.

Cover photograph by Kori Cronk Mauch of Kori Mauch Photography.

Published by Redemption Press, PO Box 427, Enumclaw, WA 98022. Toll Free (844) 2REDEEM (273-3336).

Redemption Press is honored to present this title in partnership with the author. The views expressed or implied in this work are those of the author. Redemption Press provides our imprint seal representing design excellence, creative content and high quality production.

No part of this publication may be reproduced, stored in a retrieval system, or transmitted in any way by any means—electronic, mechanical, photocopy, recording, or otherwise—without the prior permission of the copyright holder, except as provided by USA copyright law.

Unless otherwise noted, all Scriptures are taken from the Holy Bible, New International Version®, NIV®. Copyright © 1973, 1978, 1984, 2011 by Biblica, Inc.™ Used by permission of Zondervan. All rights reserved worldwide. www.zondervan.com

Scripture marked "ISV" is taken from the Holy Bible: International Standard Version®. Copyright © 1996-2007 by the ISV Foundation. Used by permission of Davidson Press, LLC. All rights reserved internationally.

ISBN 13: 978-1-63232-661-4
Library of Congress Catalog Card Number: 2014945115

This story is for every woman who has walked up to me at an event, or emailed me after reading something I've written, to tell me her story sounded so shockingly similar to mine or to say, "Thank you for your honesty," or even, "Please help me."

C.S. Lewis said, "We read to know we're not alone." Turns out, I write to know I'm not alone.

And Sweet Reader, neither are you.

ONE YEAR FROM NOW

The sanctuary feels different. The light is hurting my eyes, and it's colder. I never sit in the first row. I don't look good in black. This dress is totally inappropriate. Why didn't anyone stop me from wearing this thing? And why did I agree to have everyone over at the house after this? How am I going to pull that off?

I'm not supposed to be glad that he's dead. Okay, I guess *glad* isn't the right word. Relieved maybe?

I should probably be listening to the eulogy. *Jordan, stop messing with your tie,* I glare at my son. I can't believe he wore sneakers. And Macey, well, she's crying enough for the both of us.

I want this day to be over.

No, I'm not just relieved. I *am* glad. I'm glad my husband is dead.

ONE

NOW

I woke up on the wrong side of the bed, again. This was happening more frequently, the first thoughts that came to my mind when I woke up were a litany of all that's not right in my world, and who would want to wake up to that over and over? I would've given anything to not have to do this day of mine, wishing again to crawl right back under the covers instead. It didn't help that I was a bit foggy about last night. I absentmindedly made eggs for the kids. My breakfast of tea steeped on the counter beside me while I looked out the window at the grey mist hanging over my backyard.

Mitch was shuffling around upstairs, more than likely getting dressed. What was I going to say to him when he came down for his coffee? How did things end last night? Was it our version of fine, which would elicit a half-hearted *g'morning*? Or was it anyone's version of bad, which would find me staring into the eggs, pretending he didn't even walk into the room?

I live about fifty percent of my life all in my head, arguing with myself more than anyone else. Replaying every conversation. Correcting myself. Second-guessing myself. Wishing I'd said such-and-such instead of what I did say. Chastising myself for saying anything at all.

ONE

I heard his footsteps coming down the stairs. Think, Jules. Did you fight last night? I stirred the eggs while racking my brain. I can't remember! I quickly decided to choose neutrality over stubbornly proving a point, since I couldn't recall if I had a point to prove today.

"Morning," I said, with a small smile, looking up from the stove to Mitch.

"Morning," he replied, as he headed for the coffee pot. He poured himself a cup and walked back out of the kitchen. And that's all that we said that day.

I don't know when I last looked Mitch in the eyes. A long time ago, I memorized where that gold fleck is in his right eye. Or is it his left? But now, I not only barely look at him when he's talking to me, but if we pass each other in the hallway or if we're both in our walk-in closet at the same time, we don't even look at each other most of the time. We can even bump into each other without any recognition.

And smiling, I do that thing where I press my lips together and push my cheeks back a bit. You can't even really call it a smile. It's more of an acknowledgement that yes, I know you're here. I'm not necessarily glad you're here, but I know that you are. And to think I used to practice signing my name as his wife. What kinds of things happen that make someone change her heart like this? Innumerable, unnameable things. When did a smile become something that I decided to withhold from him? Probably around the time I started letting Mitch take little fragments of my heart without reason, without much of a fight.

I heard the clinking of keys being grabbed and the click of the lock on the front door as he closed it behind him. I felt my body and soul unclench just knowing he was out of the house. You see, I'm more me when he's not here. And I knew it wouldn't even cross my mind to miss him.

"Good morning, Mom," Macey said with her typical big smile as she walked into the kitchen about ten minutes later. She was my twin, basically. Except I wore my slightly less dark, natural red hair just past my chin in what I like to think is a very chic bob, compared to her strawberry blonde strands that flowed down her back. She lights up a room and causes something inside me to want to smile even when I feel I've got nothing to be happy about. I love that about her.

"Morning, girlie," I said to my seventeen-year-old daughter who was smiling back. "Hey, are those my boots?"

"Yeah, sorry I forgot to ask," she said sheepishly.

"No, it's not that, it's just that you tower over me in those things!" I replied with a half-hearted grin. "I made eggs for once. Can you sit for a minute?"

Macey poured herself some juice and sat down saying, "Thanks, Mom, sure. Hey, is Dad still here? He said he'd be able to give me a ride today."

"I think I heard him leave a few minutes ago ... I'm sorry," I said, sitting across from her at the table. The morning light bounced off her hair. *I wish I had that hair.* "You still have time to catch the bus, though," I consoled.

"Not really the point, is it?" asked Macey, annoyed. "Either he forgot, *again*, or he doesn't care that he makes promises that he doesn't keep."

"I know, Hon. I'm sorry," I said again, even though it wasn't my fault. I'm sort of known for apologizing for things that I didn't do. I'm working on that. "Well, maybe next time, remind him again in the morning or ..."

"Nope, no next time. I'm tired of this. What's that thing you say? Fool me once ..." she asked, not waiting for an answer. How sad that she's not learning to quote Scripture from me but instead learning the cynical phrases of love going bad—of people inevitably giving you the shaft. *Nice, Jules. Way to parent,* I thought, beating myself up.

"I gotta go. Oh, I've got student council today, so I'll be a little late. Love you, Mom," Macey said with a sigh, picking up her backpack and brushing my cheek with a kiss.

I sighed too. Another disappointment. I take on my kids' disappointments, especially those that are Mitch-induced, as if they happened to me. Small ones, big ones, they pile up around here like

ONE

junk mail, only I can't just toss them out and forget about them. They keep stacking up so high that I forget that I used to actually expect good things from time to time.

***

After getting our son, Jordan, out the door barely in time, I got on my bike to head to my father's house. *Aren't fifteen-year-olds capable of getting up and going on their own?* It was brisk and wet, the fog all but gone. I hate riding in the rain, but I do it anyway. (I do a lot of things I hate, come to think of it.)

When I was a little girl, my father would take me into the office, and I would sit under his desk and listen to the sound of the typewriters clicking away at stories for the next day's edition of the paper. I still remember his suit coat draped over my shoulders. He'd bark out orders and shoot down story ideas. I was scared of him but in awe of him all at the same time. He'd take me for bike rides, we'd go for walks. We'd go ball-hawking around the pond at the local golf course.

But when Mom died, something in him shifted, closed up maybe. Though I know he didn't stop loving me, it's like the part of him that knew how to show love evaporated. But my heart had gotten smaller too, so I almost didn't mind it that much, or even notice for that matter. At least, that's what I told my therapist all those years.

I leaned my bike up against the side of the house, just like when I was a kid. "Hey Dad," I said, knocking on the door as I opened it. He wasn't in the kitchen but the tea pot was brewing. He was expecting me. I called for him again and pulled my mug out of the cupboard. I knew where everything was because my father hadn't changed a thing. The only thing that changed is that I could reach the cupboards without the stepstool, and I didn't get to live here anymore. I had to go and grow up.

My father walked in, nodded a hello. He seemed off, fidgety maybe. "What's up, Dad?"

"Nothing," he said. He was holding a stack of mail in his hands. He looked like he was going to set it down on the table, but then turned and placed it on the counter.

"Okay," I said, not believing him. "Are you feeling alright? Did you sleep okay last night?"

"I said I'm fine." He hated all my questions. I hated all his answers.

"Alright, sorry." I poured some hot water in to my cup and sat down. The chamomile scent released and helped my shoulders untense a little.

He picked up the mail and sat down across from me, holding the letters in his lap. They were wrapped in twine, the edges yellowed. "So, are you going to tell me what those are?" I bobbed my tea bag up and down. He hesitated which made me look up at him.

"Letters from your mother," he answered sharply. "I just found them in an old box of her things."

"You *just* found them? I thought we went through the whole house right after … It's been twenty-five years, Dad," I said, not understanding.

"Twenty-six," he corrected me, pouring himself a cup of coffee. "I guess it was a box that we hadn't looked through thoroughly enough after …"

"Well, what do they say?" I asked, cutting him off, staring at the stack. "That is amazing. What does she write about? Who are they for?"

"They're for you, Jules," he said, "The whole stack. Each envelope has your name on it. They were sealed, so I didn't open them."

He's mad at me. *Hey, it's not my fault she wrote me and not you.* "For me?" I asked, sitting up in my chair and leaning forward. I looked at my father for a moment then I shifted my focus back to the letters. I wanted to grab them and run out the door, but instead I just sat there acting like I get letters from my dead mother every day.

Letters from my dead mother. Letters from my *mother*. To me. Why now? Why did my father stumble upon letters to me from Mom twenty-six years after she died? I don't believe in coincidences. If I ever needed the comfort of my mother, it would be now. You see, too much is falling apart around me. Jordan is running away from something, but I can't put my finger on what, or how to bring him back. Macey is getting ready to go away to college, and I'm not ready to let her go.

ONE

And Mitch. Well, my marriage is sometimes almost more than I can bear. So, yeah, I could probably use my mom right about now.

~~~

After making small talk with my father and gulping my tea down, I thanked him, took the letters and rode back home. Thankfully, I was in between organizing charity events. The next one was six weeks away and pretty much wrapped up already, so I didn't have to spend any time in my office prepping for it. I took a quick shower, started a fire in the fireplace, and sat down on the couch with the letters.

I held the pile in my hands for a while, feeling the weight of them, trying to let the significance sink in. I imagined Mom writing my name on each one. She was the only one who called me *Julianne*, and I loved it. It made me feel grown up. I pictured her placing each letter into the envelope and sealing it. Pictured her tying and knotting the twine around them.

I carefully untied the knot, flimsy with age. And then I counted seventeen envelopes. Seventeen. One for every year I was alive before she died.

Part of me wanted to tear into each one of them, reading every single word right then and there, soaking in all of the hoped-for wisdom, all of the longed-for comfort. But part of me wanted to savor this gift. Things like this don't just happen every day. Not to me, at least. This was heavy, deep. I was already struggling under the weight of my life and this stirred up such sadness and longing. I missed my mom desperately. I needed my mother … the real thing … not just letters from her.

I decided to read just one. Just one today. I hadn't known they existed until a couple hours ago; I didn't need to ravenously consume each word right this minute. I would spread this out, even if it killed me. "Help me be able to handle this, God," I prayed, "Whatever they say." I carefully opened the first envelope and pulled out the stationery.

> Dear Julianne,
>
> You are one year old today. I can't believe I get to be your mother! You are such a delight to me. My plan is

to write you a letter every year on your birthday and give them to you somewhere between when you turn eighteen and when you get married. We'll see. Probably depends on what I write!

You took your first step last week, and the glee on your face when you realized you were free made me laugh out loud. You are officially a handful. But you're *my* handful.

I am trying so hard to be a good wife and mother. Loving you comes naturally to me. But your father and I ... well, my darling girl, things are not always easy. He's a good man and a good provider, and he loves you so, so much.

But we're not right. Things aren't the way they're supposed to be. I know you don't notice that now, but when you look back, I can't help but wonder how much you'll remember and realize as you grow up. Did you see my tears at night? Did you hear the hushed arguments behind our bedroom door? Did you notice that your father left sometimes after an argument and didn't come back until the middle of the night? Did you ever wonder where he went? I do.

But these are not things for you now. We can talk about these things when you're older. For now, know that I love you. Know that both of us love you, and that we're trying. Even when it may not seem like we are.

And know, sweet Julianne, God loves you and will see you through anything, no matter what your life holds.

Hugs and kisses and lots of peace,

Momma

Tears slid down my cheeks. That sweeping handwriting of hers. The faintest scent of her perfume, even after all these years. *Hugs and kisses and lots of peace* ... it's what she used to say to me every night when she put me to bed. *Hugs*, a squeeze around the neck, *and kisses*, her lips would brush my forehead, *and lots of peace*, pulling the blanket

ONE

up under my chin, and then resting her hand on the top of my head as if bestowing a silent blessing.

And her admission to such unhappiness that she never let on to me when she was alive. I had no idea about my parents. "Really?" I asked myself out loud. You'd be lying if you said you didn't see all of the things she mentioned. She carried tissues with her around the house in case Dad said something to her that hurt her feelings. You knew something wasn't right.

It was too much to take. What was I supposed to do with the knowledge of my mother's pain now added on to mine? I tucked the letter back into the envelope and wrapped the string up around the bunch of letters. I held them in my lap and closed my eyes. *What does all this mean, Jesus? Why are you letting me see these now? You know how much I'm hurting right now, and now this?* I just shook my head and stood up. I put the fire out and brought the letters up to my bedroom, hiding them under my side of the bed. I washed my face and threw on a hoodie before grabbing my keys to head out. No errands, no plan of where I was going. I just needed to not be home.

I sat in Lauren's driveway, picked up my cell phone, and dialed her number. "Hello?" she answered.

"Hey, you home?" I asked.

"Yep, what's up?" she said.

"Well, I know you aren't here just to help me survive my life and everything, but can I come in? I'm sitting outside," I said sarcastically but with a quiet smile in my voice.

"Get in here," she said. She was holding the door open before I could make it up the long walk of her two-story colonial. "What's going on?" she asked, visibly concerned.

"My mom wrote me a letter," I answered as I walked through the door. "Well, a bunch of them, seventeen to be exact." I kicked off my shoes in the foyer.

"Your dead mom wrote you seventeen letters? What are you talking about?" she asked, leading me back to the kitchen. She poured me some tea without needing to ask.

"I stopped at my father's today, and he gave me a bunch of letters that he said he just found," I said. I took a sharp breath in, "The first one basically said her marriage sucked."

"Oh," Lauren said. "Wow, Honey, did you read all of them?"

"Not yet. It felt like too much. One was all I could take," I said. "What a gift, though, right? I mean, how many people get something like this? I should be happy, right?"

"Definitely … it's a gift. Well, it could be. I just hope it doesn't add to your crazy list of hard things right now," she said thoughtfully. "Speaking of too much to take, though, anything new with Mitch's situation?" she asked, leaning her elbows on the counter and resting her chin in her hands.

"Oh! I can't believe I didn't tell you this, we got word that he might be sued by both families, the pilot's and the passenger's," I responded.

"Gosh, Jules, that's horrible! How's he doing?" she asked.

"Well, he leaves every morning as if he's going to work, but I don't know where he actually goes. I don't ask him. He doesn't tell me," I laughed through tired eyes.

"Girlie, sit put," Lauren said, her arm on my shoulder. "I'm going to run you a hot bath. I was just about to do that myself, but you need it way more than I do," she insisted.

"Oh, you're too good to me," I said, "but I have to get back. Jordan will be home from school soon, and I haven't even thought about dinner yet," I said.

"Alright, but let me pray for you then," she said. "Father, this is crazy. So much stuff all at one time. Please guide Jules. Give her your strength. She needs your peace. Amen."

"Thanks," I said. We didn't say anything for a minute. I could hear the ticking of both her kitchen clock and her living room clock, not keeping time with each other. She's the only person I can be silent with and know that it's okay.

"It's all going to be okay," she said.

ONE

"I know," I said, as we each wiped a tear away.

<hr />

You're probably wondering about the thing with Mitch. He's been an air traffic controller for twenty-four years. He used to love his job. And he was the best of the best. But something started to slip. Either the stress of the job got to him or the stress of life got to his job, but he wasn't always on his game anymore.

These are not my observations, because I never saw him at work, and for some reason he stopped talking about his job a few years ago. These are statements I read in the report that he accidentally left out on his desk. An investigation was conducted regarding the night of May 26. The night a plane went down on his watch. It was a small plane, carrying a pilot and a businessman returning from a quick trip to Orlando. The toxicology report showed alcohol in his system, though he wasn't legally drunk, combined with his new antianxiety medication that I didn't know he was taking. Well, Mitch was out of it, the report said, and the rest is history. Both men were killed. He was placed on leave, and then terminated shortly after. He's been out of work for nine months. And now both families might be suing him. Correction: suing *us,* technically.

Mitch didn't come home that night until after I was asleep. But that was a normal part of our routine, either because he'd be on second shift or because he'd gone out with some guys after work for drinks. So it wasn't until the next morning that he told me what happened. Or, I should say, he told me the Mitch version of what happened. "I've got some good news and some bad news," he actually said.

"What's the good news?" I asked, wearily.

"I've got an extended vacation, starting today," he said.

I could tell, at seven o'clock in the morning, that he had already started drinking. Or perhaps, hadn't stopped since the night before. "Why?" I asked. "What's the bad news?" *Because,* I'm thinking to myself, *you, me, home ... already sounds like bad news to me.*

"There was an accident last night. A plane went down. But I don't want to talk about it, so please don't ask me any more questions." He walked away leaving me to attempt to put a thousand-piece puzzle together with only about three pieces and no picture on the box. And until the week before the trial, I wouldn't know anything else about the accident.

Mitch leaving the house each morning and not telling me where he goes is not unusual for our relationship. We don't talk about much anymore, and, come to think of it, haven't for quite a long time. Add to that my youngest being not quite right, my daughter looking for colleges, running my new business, and you could say I'm stressed. Oh yeah, and my dead mother wanting to communicate with me all of the sudden.

TWO

My Bible's on my lap but my mind is hovering on hope. If I hear one more person talk about sticky-sweet hope like it's a magic bullet, as if all I need to do is wish for it more, or just say I have it, that everything will fall into place, I'm going to have to slap that person.

Some might say my husband drinks because I'm a bitch. Others might say I'm a bitch because my husband drinks. I say it's a wash. I also say it doesn't really matter anymore, now does it? I didn't mean to grow up, marry a man who was wrong for me (and let a man marry a woman who was wrong for him, all truth be told), treat him poorly, become despairing, lose all hope time and again, and walk around with a hard, cold heart.

Most people probably don't set out to do these kinds of things, come to think of it. Picture kindergartners during finger-painting time: What do you want to be when you grow up? Oh, I don't know, but I know that I want to have a dependency on antidepressants and struggle with OCD and maybe, if I'm lucky, end up wishing my third wife would drive off a bridge. No, typically no one plots this kind of life. At least no one I know.

And yet it happens. The first part of life, we are walking along, dodging the choices that our parents have made for us, or have made for themselves that inevitably come back around and eventually smack

TWO

us in the head like a boomerang we didn't throw. The next part of our life, before we even truly know ourselves, we're making all these frightening decisions like what our career will be and whom we'll spend the rest of our lives trying to love. (But it sometimes ends up more like trying not to hate.) And the third part of our lives, which I think is where I find myself right now, is trying to live with all those choices—those both done *to* me and done *by* me.

Trying to live. Yeah, that's where I am today. Trying to strike that weird balance of being like Jesus, living out some dreams, serving others sacrificially, not being a fraud, embracing who God created me to be, not being a codependent doormat, yet not being a mean, critical, self-absorbed, cold-as-ice, causing-others-to-drink kind of woman. I stress the word *trying*.

Don't get me wrong. I believe in hope. I have a Great Hope, capital G, capital H, that one day I will see God, and he will make all things right. But I have to tell you, my experience tells me I shouldn't put too much stock in things turning out alright down here. At least, not the version of alright I'm looking for. People who follow Jesus still go bankrupt, get divorced, die from cancer, get killed in car accidents, are plagued by depression, lose friends, lose money, lose hope. We don't automatically get all our stuff straightened out down here just because … You can fill in the end of that sentence. You know what the words are. Just because we know and love Jesus and he knows and loves us … it's not a get-out-of-jail-free card. But I wanted to throw this in so you know that I am not completely hopeless. That will be important as you keep reading, because (heads-up) I'm going to act, at times, like I am totally without an ounce of hope holding me together. But in reality, hope's all I've got.

"If I lit a match in any given room in our house," I confided in a whisper to Lauren one night, "it just might explode." Tears rolled down her cheeks when I told her that.

"I had no idea," she had said.

I've been thinking about secrets. About things confessed across tables or between strangers, because strangers are safe. You can set your secret free and know it'll never come back to bite you. But this one is mine. And it bites back a lot. And this one I had kept to myself for a long, long time. Too long. I hate secrets. Really, I think there is no place for them in a marriage. Someone once told me not to overreact to the secrets and lies. I'd love to know just how they think I should react to them. Just accept them as part of life, part of the package? Just let go and let God? Just take it one freaking day at a time? Just ask Jesus to make it stop? Tried, and tried, and tried, and tried.

One of the weirdest things about this whole issue is that I was very aware of Mitch's drinking, literally from day one. But then we had Macey, and it seemed to stop. He stopped tossing six packs into the grocery cart. When I would reconcile our checkbook each month, there weren't stops at the liquor store. And the scent that had been accompanying us to bed for years disappeared. And with no explanation. In fact, once I started putting two and two together, a part of me started to relax a little bit, thinking it had all just been a really long phase, one that he was growing out of with the responsibility of fatherhood.

But the thing with secrets, they all come spilling out eventually. I heard someone say, "Truth, good. Secrets, bad." But who of us wouldn't rather step forward into the light voluntarily versus being thrust into it without warning?

So I'll start by telling on myself. My first love was Steven. My only love was Steven. We met in high school and I knew the moment I met him that I wanted to be with him for the rest of my life. The only hitch was that I was fourteen, and what did I know, really? We hung out all the time. My parents loved him. We went to youth group together. We did everything together. He was my best friend. He told

TWO

me all the time that I was beautiful, like all the time. Funny how a girl never gets sick of something like that, and I wanted to be his wife.

We dated all through high school and he got me through my mother's death right before our senior year. We went to the University of Nebraska at Omaha together, me majoring in journalism, Steven majoring in me. It wasn't until our sophomore year at college that we started sleeping together. We tried to be good and hold out, but we'd been together for so long. I think, too, that once we both got away from living with our parents, we sort of rebelled; it's just that we rebelled together.

The summer between our junior and senior year, we found out I was pregnant. I was devastated and Steven was just plain scared. We chose not to go home that summer because we were too ashamed to tell anyone, and we were trying to figure out what to do. Five weeks in, I miscarried. I have to admit, the relief I felt was unparalleled. And yet, as I cried, I knew I was crying out of loss, as well. I had lost an actual baby, and I had allowed myself to lose my innocence. I knew I would never be the same because this was the first horrible thing that happened to me, which I had done to myself.

Steven and I broke up. Not right away. We tried to stay together but we were both so broken, and we couldn't put each other back together like we'd done before. Maybe because this time, we were each other's assailants. We battled through the first half of our senior year, pummeling each other emotionally, and then something in me snapped. I decided to focus on my studies, my supposed dream of working at a major metropolitan newspaper, and I walked away from the love of my life.

I moved to Chicago right after college, somehow landed a job at the Tribune almost immediately, and left Steven behind, sort of. I only sort of left him behind because he would always have a part of my heart. He held a firm position in my memories of growing up, of being my first love, of losing my mom, and of losing my first child. You don't just forget *that* person. But I moved on, throwing myself into my job, and eventually meeting Mitch. But that wasn't the end of the Steven chapter of my life, though the moment I said, "I do" to Mitch, it should've been.

"I haven't had a drink in over six months!" Mitch yelled at me one night a few years ago. I don't even remember why we were on this topic, why I had foolishly brought it up again. "And I'm sick of you accusing me all the time and not trusting me," he pounded his hand on the kitchen counter and walked away.

I went upstairs to take a shower, to try to wash some of the argument off of me. I stopped trusting my instincts about five minutes after we got married. To this day I don't know if I'm coming or going, but only in regards to Mitch. "I'm pretty darn competent in every other area of my life," I said out loud, trying to reassure myself yet again. "But I guess I could be wrong."

Just then, I stepped down on something and felt a surge of pain shoot up my leg. *What the ...* I looked down at my foot, thinking I'd stepped on a wasp, and watched blood intermingle with the water and head to the drain. I lifted my foot to find a beer bottle cap, pointing up, at the bottom of the shower. *Six months, huh?* Tears intermingled with my blood.

When we first met, Mitch and I were so in love. Okay, not *so* in love, just in love. Or *in lust* with some *you're-so-different-than-Steven* mixed in for about fifteen minutes, twenty-some years ago.

Wait a minute, I don't even believe in being in love. I've cynically told myself for years that "it's not even in the Bible." That's me, trying to justify things. Why should I be in love with someone when it's not biblical? In other words, it's okay if you're not in love with your husband, Jules. But, mental note: you still need to, at the very least, *actions-love* him. Meaning, no one can make you feel something, including yourself, but you *can* make yourself do something, even something you don't want to do. And as we've covered, I'm pretty good at that.

TWO

Mitch and I met after college, both with fairly significant relationships and baggage trailing behind us. Though Mitch dated a lot in high school and college, he only had one other significant relationship before we met. In all the years I've known him, all I could pry out of him was that it didn't end well because she had cheated on him, and he didn't want to talk about it. And when Mitch doesn't want to talk about something, case closed.

I had just started working at the Trib and one of my first assignments was profiling high-stress jobs. Air traffic controller hit the top of the list but when I couldn't find anyone at O'Hare willing to talk with me, I started bugging people at Midway. Turns out I was either very persistent or Mitch owed his boss a favor because we ended up meeting for drinks at a dive close to the airport called Black Beetle. While waiting at the bar for Mitch to arrive, I ordered a champagne spritzer and was promptly laughed at. I turned to look behind me and saw this tall, attractive guy with piercing brown eyes extending his hand and looking me up and down. "You must be Julianne," he said with a condescending grin. "No one has ordered a spritzer of any kind in this place since … well, probably ever." I shook his hand and asked him to call me Jules. I then watched him lean against the bar, a little too close to me for a first meeting, and order two beers.

"Pretty presumptuous, don't you think?" I asked him, already slightly annoyed. "I don't drink beer."

"You do tonight," he said, placing his hand on the small of my back, guiding me to a booth in the back of the restaurant. My heart beat faster than it had since the last time I saw Steven. It was clear I missed that feeling.

Mitch's charm pulled me in. I knew I was a goner when I looked at my watch and noticed we'd been there for three hours, and I hadn't asked even one question for my article. Though it didn't slip my attention that while I nursed that one beer the entire evening, he must've ordered another four or five drinks, at some point switching to gin and tonic. It also didn't bother me in the least. And when he moved closer and said, "I've been wondering all night what it would be like to kiss you," all thoughts of unprofessionalism or me turning him down faded as he placed his hand on the back of my neck and kissed me.

And despite the faith that I had followed as a little girl, despite the fact that I didn't want to make the same mistakes I'd made with Steven, the vows made to yourself are sometimes the most difficult to keep. We went on to spend the next six months seldom apart except for work, with more and more of our belongings migrating to each other's apartments. To this day, I cannot pinpoint what the attraction was between us, because we have always been as different as night and day, with little in common. In fact, our arguing started up pretty soon in the relationship. I had never fought like this with anyone before. It felt raw and honest and harsh all at the same time. Our friends noticed it, too. No fewer than three girlfriends pulled me aside at the onset, warning me against "guys like Mitch," pointing out that he didn't seem to treat me all that well, reminding me of the long lost faith that I seemed to toss away so quickly at the first sign of male attention. One of Mitch's friends even told me at a party that he thought Mitch treated me "dirty." But I wouldn't hear any of it. Don't get me wrong. I tucked all their comments away, to pull out much later, but in the moment, they weren't saying what I wanted to hear. I didn't want to hear the truth and the truth was this—we weren't good for each other, and I should get out while I still could.

I hate replaying those conversations, because I come off as the abused girlfriend in a TV movie of the week, not that Mitch ever physically hurt me. But I would say things like, "You don't really know him like I do," and "It's not as bad as it looks," and (here's my favorite), "He really does have a faith; he's just really private about it."

Mitch's faith, well, it was pretty skin deep, and it couldn't be counted on to keep us out of trouble either. He said he was talked into going on a men's retreat in college where he accepted Jesus as his personal Savior, and he put air quotes around that phrase, but he didn't put much time or effort into that relationship until I came along. And even then, I didn't exactly roll us out of bed on Sundays to go to church while we were dating and sleeping together. It wasn't until we got married that I felt the desire—no, the *need*, a *pull*—to

TWO

get back into church and re-explore my own spiritual life. And then Mitch tagged along for appearances' sake.

But, we were each other's clean slate. We were each other's experiments in opposites not only attracting, but trying to stick it out. Apparently, I wanted to show everyone we could do it. And to prove my point, I gave him an ultimatum: Marry me, or we're done. We eloped with only his best friend from college as a witness.

We stood in front of the judge's desk in his chambers, facing each other. I reached out to hold Mitch's hand, but he put them in his pockets. I tried to catch his eye, longing for that look that every bride wishes for; the look that says I want only you, the look that says you are adored and will be forever. He looked at his shoes. He looked at the judge. He looked out the window just over my shoulder. But he never once looked me in the eye during our vows.

At the end of the night, his best man told me, through slurred words, that I'd better drive because both he and Mitch were smashed. My love for Mitch outweighed that statement, outweighed what that foreshadowed, and I took the keys with a naïve giggle, shoving the nagging feeling that I shouldn't have had to talk anyone into marrying me to the back of my mind. We called my father and his parents when we got back from our brief honeymoon in Tahoe and broke the news. No one seemed surprised, but no one seemed all that happy for us either. I tried to overlook that too.

I would be fooling myself, and you, if I claimed that something happened all of the sudden to get us to the place that we find ourselves now. There wasn't one thing. We were looking for someone to fix things in each other that a person can't fix. When a parent dies too soon, you walk around with a hole. Or at least, I did. And I wanted so desperately for Mitch to fill it. But soon after we got married, we landed in this pattern: he'd go to work then out with a couple guys for drinks. I'd go to work then come home and make dinner for myself. I'd wait up for him and he'd either get home after I was asleep, or he'd tiptoe in to find me waiting and livid. And my immaturity nudged me to start innumerable middle-of-the-night arguments with my intoxicated husband. My accusations and criticisms were taken at face value, but anyone with a bit more sobriety would have seen them for what they were ... pleas for attention, imploring him to love me, even if just a little bit.

I can now look back and see how I possibly aided in Mitch's increasing drinking habit, though it's taken the distance of years and years to admit it. But I have to say it: I *was* a pill. I'm not saying I'm not anymore, by any means, though I'd like to think I'm a bit easier to swallow these days.

One of our first married blowouts was epic. It was a brutally cold January evening, and we were driving to church of all places. I was making him go. But by the time we were halfway there, neither of us wanted to continue because our fight had escalated. At one point, I yelled, "Pull over and let me out!" I think I'd seen that in a movie or something, except in the movie, that line worked to soften the heart of the guy and they made up. Only problem, this wasn't a movie. Because the moment I said that, Mitch slammed on the brakes and pulled over, reaching across me to open up my door. Well, I would not be made even bigger of a fool by recanting, so I got out and started walking home. I wanted to kill him. I wanted to die. I wanted out. The wind and darkness swirled around me with each passing, speeding car, and I actually feared for my life on that busy road. But I kept walking, dammit. About five minutes later, he pulled up behind me and told me to get in. I did, but with great internal hesitance. I knew if I got in, he would win. I'm not sure what, but I knew I'd be on the losing end of this one, and probably the next few. But I got in and didn't say another word to him for days. Come to think of it, that's when his drinking started up again.

Just after I had Macey, I found myself completely out of sorts. Mitch had always been an anger trigger for me before, and then I couldn't seem to get a handle on my emotions, though at the time, I couldn't see it. I was raging through one argument over a broken promise, but let me point out how small the promise was—he had promised to return a phone call and then forgot. The point between knowing I was losing control and actually losing control grew fuzzy,

TWO

and all I remember is shoving Mitch with all my weight into the doorjamb of our bathroom.

He staggered back and looked at me almost in shock. Eyes narrowed, he said, "Never, ever touch me like that again," and he stormed out.

I was dizzy. I couldn't believe I had just done that. I had never done anything like that to anyone. And all I could think was, "If only he didn't drive me so crazy …" I'm not even sure I apologized to him. But I sure do remember journaling the next morning how he came home the night before drunk again. Forget my eyes, my life was filled with planks and logs, and I was piling them up like excuses of my own.

We circled in and out of this pattern for several years, until the kids came along, and I was just too tired to stay up any more—too tired to fight as much anymore. So, things quieted down somewhat. But don't get me wrong, the quiet was not equated with things getting better or even my acceptance of reality, as I believe Mitch assumed. It simply meant I had started to give up. A girl giving up is a really sad sight.

And so we clawed and scratched our way through, unhappily up to this point. And here we are now, two kids and twenty-two years later, barely hanging on by a thread. It's not that Mitch is a bad man. And it's not that I'm a saint. But together, well, together we hurt each other in ways we wouldn't dream of hurting anyone else. We say things, we do things, we *don't* say things, we *don't* do things. Throw in an evolving addiction and basically there's a lot of damage being done on a regular basis.

I used to count the hours until I would see Mitch again … literally, on a piece of monogrammed stationery next to my computer at work. I hid it, of course, because, can you even imagine the ridicule I would've had to endure at the paper from my co-workers? Now I count the hours until he leaves the house. Just in my head. I wouldn't want him to stumble upon that, which would stir up an entirely different level of ridicule.

THREE

"*It just doesn't feel right,*" he said. This was Mitch trying to break up with me, a few months into our relationship.

"How are we supposed to know what right feels like," I asked. And this was my odd attempt at convincing him not to.

After the initial lust wore off, things were tenuous and hard—harder than hard should be in a new relationship. But I didn't know that. Or, if I knew, I didn't want to acknowledge it. But, Mitch felt it. And I think he was not only trying to get out while he could for his own sake, but I think he was trying to spare me some future pain as well. It was actually one of the most gallant things he'd end up ever trying to do for our relationship. "I think we might be a square peg and a round hole," he told me, holding my hand, sitting next to me on the couch.

Something in me rose up. It was the part of me that I tried to keep pushed down at all times, that lived inside me and drove me to make horrible decisions. It was the part of me that was just waiting for someone, every person I ever met, to confirm that there was something inherently wrong with me, and I wasn't quite up to par for being in a partnership. It would sneak out every time I turned in an assignment, in those hours where I waited for my editor's feedback. It would taunt me, telling me my journalism skills were disastrous at best, and nil at worst. It would hover just under the surface between every first and

THREE

second date I'd ever had; and when the second date didn't come to pass, it would sneer, "I knew it. I told you so."

So when Mitch came to me that day and said, "I think we'd be better off apart," this is what I heard: "I think I'd be better off not having you in my life because you are just too needy and dependent, and you scare the crap out of me, and I think you'll bleed me dry emotionally." I also heard, "And I think you should get used to the fact that no one will ever be able to love you the way you are, so you might want to start acting like you're something else."

That monster in me heard those words and laughed, "What did I tell you? You are unlovable." So, I pushed the monster back down with words like, "I'll be better, Mitch, I promise. I'll stop arguing with you. I'll stop yelling. I'll stop calling as much. You can hang out with your friends as much as you want. You can do whatever you want. You can see me only when you want to see me. Please, please don't break up with me." *Please. I'm begging you. I need you. I may not want you. I may not love you. I may agree that we're really terrible together. But I need you. Don't leave me. Please.*

With those words, I quieted the monster, for a time, and I convinced Mitch, for a time. We didn't break up that day. But I would always, always know deep down that we should have.

My journal was slowly becoming my best friend.

> God, you know, there are moments when I have this sense of expectation. But it is far away and undependable. It scares me, too, because it's not a deep hope in what you can do in my marriage or in Mitch's life, or even in my heart or my life. To be really honest, I gave up on all that a long time ago.
>
> What it is that scares me is a flicker of a promise that no one has ever made me, that one day, I will be free of this. And I don't mean one day in heaven, but one day here on earth. That somehow, I will be free of my marriage,

however that may look, and I will know what it is like to be loved by a healthy, whole, holy, actual human man who knows and speaks his emotions and thinks I'm absolutely something to behold. Someone who doesn't need an elixir to be with me. I shouldn't hang my hat on that, because, odds are, it's not going to happen. The odds are not in my favor on this one.

I am waiting for you to end my marriage, Lord. That's what I'm waiting for. I am waiting for things, not just wanting but waiting for, things I should not be entertaining. My hope, bottom line, should be in you carrying me through in who you are, but I confess that it's not. Today, these days, my hope is a lower-case hope based on very selfish things. I am sorry.

When Macey was four years old and Jordan just one, I received an email at work. It was brief, but rocked my little world.

> Julie,
> I miss you. I haven't married. I'm still waiting for you. Please call me.
>   Steven

The timing was either superb or horrible, depending on your viewpoint. My desolation had left me inconsolable and paralyzed. No one would've ever guessed that to look at me. I was attempting to be the ultimate working mother while my marriage was taking its time dying in clamorous yet imperceptible ways. I was doing too much, tired all the time, and dangerously desperate for affirmation.

I remember hearing that an unsatisfied soul is a problem waiting to happen. I wrote in my journal:

> Jesus, I am not satisfied. I am lonely. I am empty. I am not loved. I am vulnerable. Please, please fill me up with you. I want to want you more than I want to be genuinely loved by a man. I'm not there yet, but I want to want this. Please

THREE

help me want you more. Please meet all of my needs in you. Please give me more and more of you.

But without leaning on the strength that I was supposed to have in Christ, and without so much as letting the ink dry in my journal, I called Steven. Years before, sometime between falling for Mitch and realizing I should walk away, I ran into Steven. We were both driving on the interstate, and I saw his car up ahead of me. I don't know what got into me but I sped up so we were side by side. I didn't look over at him, but wanted him to notice me. Once I realized he did, I took off. I let him chase me, weaving in and out of the lanes of traffic. I let him catch up to me, and then acted surprised when he pulled alongside me. He motioned for me to get off at the next exit, and I followed him.

It had been ages since we'd seen each other, let alone had a conversation, but the moment he reached me, he pulled me out of my car and then pushed me up against it with his whole body, his mouth landing on mine. He stopped only to say, "I would have chased you halfway across the state." I forgot where I was. I forgot we were standing next to a car on the side of a busy road, with my wedding dress in the backseat. I wanted to abandon my car right there, abandon my life right then, and take off with him. But I didn't. I drove back home. I married Mitch.

And then the email, years later. We began an affair that filled a hole inside of me I hadn't realized was so deep. Something I should point out is that he remained in Nebraska, and we never actually saw each other. I went so far as to plan a weekend away to meet up with him under the guise of a writing assignment, but I chickened out at the last minute. However, we had rekindled that friendship that had meant so much to me all those years before and that I had been missing in my marriage. I allowed myself to love him again, to love him still, even in two short months, sharing my heart with another man besides my husband.

At first, I didn't feel even a single pang of guilt. I was excited and filled up and oddly free. I felt confident again, someone loved me. *Me.* He didn't criticize me. He didn't tell me all the ways I should be doing things differently or better. He didn't ignore me. Someone had been waiting for *me*, had missed *me*. I felt loved. Pursued.

But then I made the mistake of sharing this with Lauren. I believe others might refer to this as divine intervention. Lauren, whom I trusted completely, gave me an ultimatum: I either had to end it with Steven and confess the whole thing to Mitch, or she would tell Mitch herself. I was beside myself. I couldn't believe she was doing this to me but I relented. I had been fooling myself. What was going on with Steven was a holding on to history. It was an escape. And (I so hated to admit this), it was sin.

I wrote him an email as brief as the one that started it all.

> Steven,
> I can't keep doing this. I am married. This is wrong.
> Please don't contact me anymore.
>
> Julianne

And he never did. I mourned the ending of that relationship, but more than just because I was missing Steven. Part of me had felt that he just might be my out, or at least a temporary departure from my reality. And he had been. But I needed to move on and face up to the facts. I remember the day that I confessed to Mitch as if it just happened five minutes ago. The kids were playing in the living room, and he and I were in the kitchen.

"I have something I need to tell you," I said in hushed tones. "I've been doing something behind your back, something I'm ashamed of," I continued, not looking him in the eyes.

"What is it?" he asked, moving closer to me.

"Steven contacted me a couple months ago and we've been … talking," I said. I looked at him, "More than talking. I almost went away with him," I said looking away again, cringing as if I were about to be slapped.

Mitch didn't respond. He just stood there, looking past me now, just over my shoulder to the kids.

"I'm so sorry," I said through tears. "I've been so lonely, but I know now that it was a mistake, and I will never do anything like that

THREE

again," I said. "Can you forgive me, Mitch?" I asked him. He didn't react the way I had thought he would, or hoped. Deep down, I was hoping for a jealous rage, some sign of life, some flicker that there was still love underneath all of the piling up wreckage.

In spite of my tears, my genuine remorse, he said evenly, sharply, "If he still wants you, he can have you," and he walked out. Devastated by the lack of grace, by the lack of love, I packed up Macey and Jordan and went to stay with Lauren for a few days. I hoped I'd be missed, and that maybe he just needed some time to cool off.

That was sixteen years ago. Something in my world split open that day, the day my husband told me that another man could have me, that he didn't want me enough to fight for me. The split was never able to be put back together again.

My world had split open when my mother died, when I found out I was pregnant at nineteen, when I miscarried, when Steven and I broke up, and then again with Mitch's declaration. And I was beginning to suspect that it is what life is all about, your world splitting open, again and again.

All I know is that throughout the past twenty-two years, there have been days I wish I weren't married to Mitch, days I wish I weren't married at all, days I can't believe we have stayed married this long, days I wish I hadn't cancelled that weekend away after all. Then there are days when so much else is going on that my marriage is the least of my problems.

FOUR

MY FATHER WAS A STAUNCH conservative who happened to marry a Jesus-loving hippie. Looking back now, they made the oddest pairing, which is more than likely where I got my proclivity for opposites attracting. And when I was a little girl, I couldn't wait to grow up and have what I thought they had. We went to church every Sunday, but I asked Jesus to come into my heart when I was nine, on my mom's bed. She was combing out my long, tangled hair after a bath, getting ready to braid it, and I asked her why she loved Jesus when he's invisible. I think I thought he was like the tooth fairy or something.

She kept brushing my hair, longer than she needed to because she was in thought. I'm sure she was trying to figure out how to put her grown-up faith into nine-year-old words, so she said, "I've never been loved by anyone the way I'm loved by Jesus." She had to set my hairbrush down to get a tissue.

"I didn't mean to make you cry, Mommy," I said.

"Oh, Honey, you didn't. You just asked a really good question and it helped me remember something that I haven't remembered in a little while. So thank you actually," she said with a quiet laugh. Then I asked her how I could feel that love and she led me in a prayer right then and there, kneeling on the floor next to her bed, me with only one braid done.

FOUR

I didn't know then that I would go on to stop and start to feel God's love for most of my life, only coming to find out much later in life that every time I felt the love slip away, it was actually me walking away in some form or another, with only the very occasional absence being on God's part. But mostly, it was me.

~~~~~

Mitch walked in just as I was pulling dinner out of the oven. Macey was setting the table and Jordan was getting our drinks.

"You were supposed to take me to school today, Dad," Macey said.

"I forgot," Mitch said, looking through the mail without even a hint of an apology.

"Oh, okay, I forgive you. Sure I understand, you *forgot*," Macey replied sarcastically.

I glanced at her. "Don't be disrespectful, Mace," I said.

"Sorry," she said reluctantly as she sat down.

"Joining us for dinner?" I asked Mitch as I sat down at the table.

"I'm here, aren't I?" he responded while tossing the mail back down.

Breathe, I told myself. *Just let that one go. He's under a lot of stress.* "Good," I said with a fake smile, pulling an extra plate out, wishing I could chuck it at his head just this once. I set the plate down and looked at my kids. We used to do one of those question books around the dinner table. You know, the ones that ask things like: If you had one book to read for the rest of your life, what would it be and why? But here's the question I inevitably get every time: If you had to live on a deserted island forever, what one person would you bring?

I wouldn't choose Mitch. But I feel contractually obligated to do so, or at least to say so if one of my kids happens to be the one doing the asking. How do you choose between two kids? Can't. I'd probably pick Lauren, but that would be weird to say out loud. And it might hurt everyone's feelings. So I usually say *Jesus*. I know he'd be with me anyway but saying *Jesus* saved me from a lot of awkward conversations.

I watched a close friend in college meet, be courted by, fall in love with (for lack of a better phrase that I actually believe in), and marry her husband. They are one of those couples where I cannot picture any other person who would fit as perfectly with either of them. They were, cliché intentional, made for each other. They are each other's favorite person. And then it hit me: *I'm nobody's favorite person.*

I was snapped back into the present with Macey saying, "High/low, everybody! Oh, and one way you brought glory to God today. Our youth group is doing this together."

Jordan, "High: I got a B+ on my math test. Low: I pulled a muscle in gym. Glory to God: I didn't swear when I pulled that muscle," he said, rolling his eyes.

Mitch laughed.

"*Okay* ... good," I said, with a half-smile. "That's a start."

Macey went next. "My low was that I got my schedule from work, and I'm on for a fourth weekend in a row. But my high: I got accepted to the University of Nebraska! I've been dying to tell you guys!"

"Honey, that's wonderful!" I said, giving her a hug. "We're so proud of you, right Mitch?" I asked him.

"Yeah, Macey, that's really great," he said. "That's my girl."

"I still don't know where I'm going to go yet, but it's cool to start thinking about it. Oh, and I brought glory to God by staying after the student council meeting to talk with Tara about her parents' divorce. She's having a pretty hard time with it," she said.

"You're such a good friend, Honey," I said. "Mitch, you want to go next?" I asked, trying not to come across as a nag.

"My high was the guy at Starbucks accidentally giving me a Grande instead of a Tall and not charging me extra. My low was something at work," he said while shooting me a look as if to say, *keep your mouth shut.* Or at least, that's how I interpreted the look. I wanted to scream, *just tell the kids the whole truth!* I hate living in lies and secrets.

Macey said, "Dad, you didn't say how you brought glory to God today."

"Ummm," he started, thinking, "I helped a lady change her flat tire this morning."

"Wow, Dad, that's great," Macey said with a big smile.

FOUR

"Yeah," I nodded half-heartedly. *A real Good Samaritan*, I thought sarcastically to myself. *Jules, come on, you criticize him even when he's done something good. Can he ever win?* I argued with myself.

"Go, Mom, so I can head out," Jordan said.

"Gee, thanks for the huge interest in my life, Jor," I laughed. "Okay, well, my high pretty much eclipsed anything else for the day today. Grandpa found a pile of letters from my mom that she had written to me, and so I read one of them this morning. Pretty intense," I finished, looking around the table for some kind of affirmation. I was hoping Mitch would ask me questions, show some interest. Instead, he stood up, picked up his plate and put it next to the sink.

"I've got some things to do in town. I might be home late," he said as he walked out of the kitchen without an actual goodbye.

With that, Jordan was up as well. "Cool about the letters, Mom. I'm meeting Drew at the park. I'll be back before dark," he said.

"Do you have homework?" I started to ask, but he was already out the door.

"I'll help with dishes, Mom," Macey said. "So, what did the letter from Grandma say? Can I read it?"

"Oh," I said. It hadn't occurred to me that I'd be asked about the content. "Umm, I don't think they're going to be quite appropriate for you to read yet, Hon, but it's just basically stuff about me growing up."

"What could be so inappropriate about you growing up?" she asked me. "Let me guess," she finished, "it's a long story?" She flashed me that cute grin of hers. She knows me so well.

"Pretty much," I said. "Go ahead, I've got the rest," I said, taking the dishtowel from her hand.

Yeah, it's a long story.

<hr>

"How does that make you feel?" I asked Mitch just before we got married, over something benign that I can't even remember now.

His response, "If I ever figure out how I feel on any given topic, I promise you'll be the first to know."

Red flag number thirty-seven.

"Why do you still make me drive all the way out here to meet you for a drink when you're not even working out here right now?" Greg asked Mitch, as he sat down next to him at the bar.

"What can I say? I like what I like," Mitch smiled. "Two more," he said to the bartender.

"So, what's up?" Greg asked.

"Nothing really. I just needed to get out of the house," Mitch said.

"You been here long already?" Greg asked.

"What do you care?" Mitch demanded, taking a drink of his gin and tonic.

"Geez, Mitch, I was just asking," Greg answered. "So, why do you need to get out of the house so badly?"

"That damned Jules. She's always getting on my case. Like I don't have enough on my mind these days," he snarled. "I'm telling you, she drives me crazy sometimes. If it weren't for her, I sure wouldn't be spending so much time here."

"Really?" Greg asked, his voice dripping in sarcasm. "She drives you here and pours gin down your throat, does she?" he asked, shaking his head in disapproval.

"Who the hell do you think you are, Mr. High and Mighty all of the sudden?" Mitch said, standing up, accidentally knocking over his bar stool.

The bartender and other patrons looked over.

"Mitch, calm down," Greg said. "I'm just saying, I think you pretty much have dug your own grave, man. No woman can be so bad to do this to someone," he said.

"Go home, Greg. Okay? Just leave me alone. I'm sorry I called you," Mitch said, picking up the stool and sitting back down again. He finished his drink in one gulp and asked for another.

"Let me take you home, Mitch," Greg said, grabbing Mitch's upper arm. "You're done for today," he insisted.

"Get off me. And don't tell me what to do," he said, pushing Greg's hand away. Greg reached across the bar in front of Mitch and grabbed

FOUR

his car keys. Mitch didn't fight him. Greg walked outside and made a call.

I went to bed late and then couldn't fall asleep, obsessing for a good hour. Where was Mitch, and what was he doing? Then, I began praying that if he were out drinking, that he'd get pulled over, get a DUI, be taken in, would call me to come bail him out, and I would say no and quietly hang up. And part of me was hoping that he would not make it home at all. But I couldn't help but wonder, what kind of Jesus-follower hopes her husband dies? *A really sad one* was the only answer I could come up with.

Just then, the phone rang, startling me from my half-sleep. "Hello?" I answered quietly.

"Jules, it's me, Greg," he shouted.

"Greg? I can hardly hear you. Where are you?" I asked.

"We're at Black Beetle," he said. "Listen, you need to come get Mitch. He's had too much, and I took his keys."

"Greg, why can't you just drive him home?" I asked, not bothering to hide my irritation.

"He says he doesn't want to leave his car here overnight," Greg explained.

"Well, you know what? He should've thought about that before he got drunk again," I said. "I'm not coming to get him, Greg. Either you can bring him home, he can take a cab, or he can sleep in his car, but he's on his own tonight," I said, hanging up. *Was that mean of me?* I thought. At this point, I didn't care.

I sat up in bed and turned on the lamp on my nightstand. My eyes adjusted to the light and landed on a picture of the four of us together at the beach when the kids were small. Mitch was holding my hand, and we were both laughing at something I no longer remember. I love and hate that picture for the same reason. It isn't the real us.

I reached underneath my bed and pulled out the pile of Mom's letters. I undid the twine again and opened the next one. It was more of the same. She was glad to be my mother; I was running all over the place and saying no constantly at the age of two. I read the third and fourth, my eyes getting heavy. But something in the fifth one caught my eye.

> Oh, Julianne, you walked in on an argument between your father and me and you started to cry. It broke my heart. I had been so careful up to this point, arguing in our bedroom or in whispered tones, but this time we slipped. I'm so sorry. You even asked us to stop yelling at each other.
>
> The Richardsons— you know them, my darling, because you are in kindergarten with their son, Bobby— are getting a divorce. In fact, seems like half the couples we know are divorcing. At least someone's getting free.

At least someone's getting free? My mother was longing for freedom too. Her words didn't bring me the consolation I was hoping for. They simply made me even sadder, and the weight on my shoulders loomed larger. I hated thinking about her in such pain, realizing that my childhood was shrouded in secrecy and unfulfilled longings. "Just like my adulthood, and my children's childhoods for that matter," I said out loud to the air.

The only people who actually believe that kids are resilient are the adults who are trying to justify what they did to them. I recall the argument my mother wrote about. I had just come in from playing outside, but my parents must not have heard the kitchen door open. I could hear them in the other room, both yelling, neither listening to the other. I stood in the doorway and watched in silence. My powerful father and my carefree mother seemed to blend into the same person. Yelling shrunk them both down to the same thing. I started to cry but they still didn't see me or hear me. I grabbed a paper napkin from the counter and started to shred it in pieces. It was just the three of us, so when the two of them were mad at each other, everything seemed wrong. I don't remember any of the words, I just remember the feeling. It felt like I was being pulled away from them. At one point, my father held my mother's shoulders in his hands and he was

FOUR

shaking her while she cried. That's when I recall them both turning to look in my direction, but I didn't know why. I must've yelled at them to stop, like my mother said in the letter, which is so odd because I had felt like I was in a dream when you can't say or do anything, when you feel the need to yell but no sound comes. Something in my little mind switched that day, and I decided I would never feel incapable of expressing myself again. No matter what that would mean. I just didn't know I was committing to expressing myself at the expense of others.

I heard the garage door open around one. Mitch had made it home. My selfish prayer was not answered. My yearning for freedom was shelved for another day. I quickly tied up the letters and placed them back under the bed, then turned off the light and settled myself. He announced to all that he was home by dropping his keys and some coins on the stairs on his way up. He got undressed in the dark, knocking into the dresser. The smell of alcohol shocked my senses completely. I remained still, though, not wanting him to know I was awake. He climbed into bed and rested his hand on my hip. He moved his hand down and reached between my legs.

Between the scent that I had come to loathe and the current status of our relationship, I was flooded with thoughts. How do I respond to his touch? Do I yell at him and list off all the reasons I can't even imagine having sex with him right now? Or do I acquiesce out of duty's sake? I couldn't decide what to say or what to do, so I did nothing, pretending I was asleep by slowing my breathing. Within moments, his hand fell away and I heard his steady breathing turn into a snore.

Crisis averted, I thought to myself. *This time, at least.*

In a state of intoxication Mitch once told me that he started drinking again as a "barometer of our relationship." I may have been a trigger early on, I get that. I was no peach to be married to. But I ran across a saying on a website that maybe he hasn't heard just yet: I didn't cause it, I can't control it, and I can't cure it.

I AM NOT THE REASON YOU DRINK! YOU ARE. STOP BLAMING ME! I want to scream. I want to write this on the mirror for him to find after a shower. But I don't, because maybe it really is my fault after all. Who's to say?

FIVE

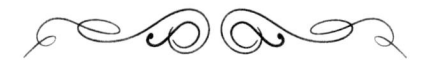

MITCH DIDN'T SPEAK TO ME for sixteen days one time. My first mistake was having a thought that contradicted his. My second mistake was actually telling him. My final mistake was not backing down once I realized mistakes one and two.

I had told him that I didn't think it wise that he drink before going into work. I know, crazy, right? This was years ago. I then told him that I was going to ask Greg to back me up on this if he didn't stop. "Mitch, for goodness' sakes, you shouldn't even be *driving* when you drink, let alone trying to navigate airplanes all over Chicagoland." I was pretty convinced I was right. The only part that I was unsure about was that I had no evidence of his actually drinking, you know, other than all his tells. I saw no actual alcohol to back it up, but still.

He yelled at me for a while, and when I said I wasn't changing my mind, he looked at me a good long time and walked out of the room. He didn't say even one word to me for sixteen days. He'd occasionally send a message through Macey, but he pretty much just acted like I didn't exist. For instance, it used to be that whoever goes to the bathroom first put toothpaste on both of our toothbrushes as a habit. There was no toothpaste on my toothbrush for sixteen days.

I even had minor surgery during that time, and not only did he not take me to the hospital or back, he didn't even ask me how it went. Seriously? Later, when he lifted his talking ban, he accused me

FIVE

of purposely scheduling it during that time to try to get attention. Yep, sounds totally like something I'd do, "schedule" an emergency appendectomy in exchange for a few words from my husband.

Ask me why he started talking to me again. He got a DUI and had to call me to pick him up at the police station. And even then, his first words to me were, "What took you so long to get here?"

We were sitting in the kitchen one Sunday afternoon reading the paper when Mitch asked me the strangest question. "What would your ideal marriage look like?"

I think I choked on my tea. "You want to know how I'd like our marriage to be?" I asked, clarifying for both our benefit.

"Yes," he answered. "Actually, I'd like you to write it down and give me the list." I rolled my eyes.

"I'll think about it," I said nonchalantly, like I thought it was a petty request. But inside, I was jumping up and down. Finally my chance to put on paper my deepest desires and to have them be known by my husband. I couldn't wait. This is what I came up with:

> Loving Jesus together would be our highest priority.
> Our kids would feel loved and secure.
> We would be each other's closest friend.
> Alcohol would not be the third party in our marriage.
> We would trust each other.
> We would tell each other the truth at all times.
> There would be no secrets.
> Arguments would be resolved calmly and respectfully.
> I would not cry myself to sleep over the state of our marriage or out of loneliness.
> We would have goals and dreams for our future.
> I want to be with someone who thinks I am amazing, who can't believe he gets to be with me, who knows me well, who supports me in my dreams, who encourages me, who thinks I'm quirky but not in need of a complete

overhaul. In other words, who really, really loves me and really, really likes me.

Was I asking a lot? Perhaps. Was I asking for things that no one else has? No. I'd seen real life marriages just like this. But was I asking too much of us? Does it matter really?
The next day, "Here's that list."
"What list?" he asked me.
"The list of things I want to see in our marriage. You asked me to do this yesterday," I explained, realizing that he didn't remember either because he was intoxicated yesterday, he's intoxicated now, or both.
"You know I don't read anything you write, Jules."
I inhaled so deeply, his words caught in my throat. I wanted to feel the shards as they went down, I wanted to digest them. I threw the list at him and walked away. I live and breathe on self-justification. I must admit, though, despite the innumerable disappointments up to that point, I had held out a small slice of expectation. I had pinned a heck of a lot of hope on him holding in his hands my wishes and desires. I mean, he had asked me for it, even if he forgot that he did. That was something, wasn't it? But then a few days later, I found it crinkled up in a ball on the floor of his office.
I felt like I was in *The Wizard of Oz* when the tornado is coming, the wind is whipping everything around, and they are calling for Dorothy to run to the cellar, but they have to shut the door because the tornado is bearing down on them. My heart was that cellar and seeing that piece of paper balled up on the floor was like the wind of the tornado slapping the cellar door shut. He had basically asked to see my heart, and I had given it to him in black and white, only to have it wind up on the floor. *Never again*, I told myself, never again.

I walked past Macey's room and saw her propped up on her bed, journal in hand. "Hey, Hon," I said, leaning against the doorway. "Can I come in?" I asked.

FIVE

"Sure," Macey said with a small sigh.

"What's on your mind?" I asked her, discerning some sadness in her eyes. Macey closed her journal and set it on the bed next to her. *She is so beautiful. And she keeps so much in. I hope she shares her heart with me ... or at least, I hope she's sharing it with you, Lord.* I prayed silently.

"A lot," she said. "Things seem ... upside down ... but I don't even know why."

"Is it school? Work? College decision stuff?" I asked. *Please don't say it's home.*

"No, I don't think so. I mean, school's hard but I'm doing pretty well. And work is just, well, work. And sure I'm a little confused about college but ... well, things around here seem less right than usual," she said.

Less right than usual? My sweet girl. I'm so sorry you have to grow up in a family that you know is not right, I thought, but didn't say.

"Just thinking about Daddy," she continued. It melts my heart that at seventeen, she still calls her father, Daddy. I sat, letting her continue, reaching out to push some hair back behind her ear. "Where does he go every day?" she asked me.

"What do you mean?" I replied, trying to hide my surprise at her question. I wasn't prepared for this conversation.

"I'm not stupid. *We're* not stupid," she added. "Jordan and I know that something's up with Dad's work, that he hasn't been going there for months," she said diplomatically.

"Oh ... ummm ... listen, Mace," I stalled, "this is really a question for you to pose to your dad," I answered, knowing her well enough to know that it wouldn't appease her.

"Really?" she asked. "You think he's actually going to give me a straight answer to that question?" she asked. I guess we all know each other pretty well around here. "That's why I asked you instead of him," she replied with a smug smile.

"Well," I started to say, but she interrupted. "And while we're on the subject," she said, "is it my imagination or does he seem ... what's the word I'm looking for? *Off* lately?"

"What do you mean by 'off'?" I asked, not liking where this chat was going. I wanted Macey to feel she could talk to me about anything, but we were getting into dangerous territory here. Mitch wouldn't even tell *me* where he went every day, would never agree to tell the kids about his job situation, and hadn't ever admitted to drinking again. What in the world was I supposed to tell our daughter?

"I mean, when I talk to him sometimes, it's like he's only half there. And his mood swings, sometimes he's all happy, and sometimes he looks like he wants to punch a hole in the wall," she answered me with a well-thought-out response.

"Oh *that*," I said lightly, and we both giggled, breaking up the tension a bit. "What do *you* think it is?" I asked, pulling out all my parenting skills in one conversation. In other words, stalling again.

"If I knew, Mom, I wouldn't be asking," she responded. Her eyes narrowed and she began to speak again but stopped herself.

"What?" I asked.

"Well, you know my friend, Tara, whose parents are divorcing?" she asked me.

"Yes," I said, really hoping she was changing the subject onto someone else's family problems.

"She was telling me that one of the reasons they're getting a divorce is because her mother has a drinking problem. And some of the things she said that her mom has done, and how she acts, sort of sound like Dad to me," she finished. She looked at me, probably waiting for a quick denial on my part.

"Honey," I replied, "things are complicated right now." I reached for her hand. "I want you to know that you can talk to me about anything and that when I can, when it's appropriate, I want to be able to answer all your questions. But what you've just asked me, well, I can't talk to you about it right now," I said. "I'm sorry and I hope you understand."

"I don't understand. We're a family," she said. "I should be able to know what's going on." Then she continued, "Never mind. I don't like it, but if you're saying you can't talk about it, I'll try to respect that," she responded.

FIVE

"Good. Thank you, Honey," I said. "I'm really sorry; please know that I wish I could." I stood up to leave, reaching down to kiss her on the top of her head.

"Mom," she said, stopping me from going, "I hate secrets."

"Oh, Macey, me too. I hate secrets too," I said, nodding my head, and turned and walked out.

Jesus, I am so controlling. I think I'm getting better as I get older but it's hard for me to just let go and let people make their own choices, especially when those choices are clearly mistakes. My children have suffered at the hand of my tight grip, as has Mitch. More than I'd like to admit. But I've noticed as my kids have gotten older that I don't just have my hands in their individual lives, but in their relationships, with each other and with Mitch. And I don't want to do that anymore.

I read somewhere that every adult is 100 percent responsible for each of their relationships. So I'm trying to step away, to step out. It isn't easy though, especially when I hear one of the kids in a crazy-making conversation with their father, while he's slightly inebriated, holding a cup of gin that they think is water. It takes everything in me in those moments to not barge in and to keep my mouth shut. But then I wonder: Is that what a responsible parent should do? Should I let them flounder, letting them possibly think that they're the crazy ones? Have I mentioned that I hate this? Have I mentioned that I need your help?

"So, what do all the letters say?" my father asked during a visit. We sat across the kitchen table from each other, each with our mugs in our hands. We both fidgeted with our cups while we waited for my answer.

"Oh, you know, just stuff about me growing up, Dad," I responded, hoping he'd drop the subject. He didn't.

"Your mother say anything about us?" he pried.

"About *us*?" I asked, feigning innocence.

"About your mother and me," he clarified impatiently.

"A little bit. I haven't read them all yet. I'm sort of pacing myself," I said.

"Well, there's two sides to every story," my father said. "I just wanted you to know that."

"I know, Dad," I responded.

But I didn't know. I wanted to ask him what that meant, but I didn't want to tip him off about how much Mom was sharing in these letters to me. Besides, I was in a story of my own, and I hated thinking about there being another side besides mine. It was easier to just assume that my version of my life was gospel truth and everyone else was wrong.

Back home, I stood quietly at the living room doorway, trying to size up the situation. Should I go in and talk to Mitch or not? I would just be putting off a conversation I felt I needed to have if I walked away, so I headed over to him to get the thing over with.

"So, anything new about the case?" I asked Mitch, standing next to the couch where he was sprawled out. He put down the paper.

"I'm meeting with the lawyer tomorrow. Why?" he asked.

"I was just checking in, no specific reason," I replied. "I just like knowing what's going on," I added. He didn't say anything but looked up at me like, *well?*

"Mitch, we need to talk," I said. "Can I sit down for a minute?" He didn't move the paper for me to sit down, so I just leaned on the armrest.

"About what?" he asked defensively. I don't blame him. It's rare that I broach a conversation with him that isn't loaded emotionally with some criticism or accusation. I'm working on it, just not today.

FIVE

"Macey asked me where you go every day," I answered. "She said that she and Jordan aren't stupid and know that something's up."

"And what did you tell her?" he blamed.

"I told her that was a subject she needed to bring up with you," I answered, my turn to be defensive.

"Really? You didn't spill all the details?" he accused.

"No, Mitch, because first of all, I don't even know all the details. And believe it or not, I'm not the enemy here. I really do think this is your news to tell. And I've been trying to honor you by keeping my mouth shut this whole time, but the kids know something's up. So, I really think you should sit down with both of them and tell them what's going on," I said. "And I think you'll be surprised by their response to you," I added. "I don't think you're giving them enough credit. They're your kids, and they love you, Mitch," I finished.

"I'll think about it," he said.

"If Macey asks me again," I added, pushing, "what do you want me to tell her?"

"Nothing. Tell her nothing. And if you do, you'll be bringing Satan into our family."

"*What?* What are you talking about?"

"If you go against my authority as the head of the home, you will be bringing Satan into our family."

He stood up to leave the room. "You know what, on second thought, you go right ahead." He was taunting me. He turned back around, looked directly at me with anger in his eyes, and said, "Actually, I don't care. You can tell her everything. Do whatever you want. You always do anyway."

"Do whatever I want? Are you kidding me?" I yelled. "Stay right here," I said and walked over to the fireplace. I grabbed the eleven-by-fourteen portrait off the wall and walked back over to him, carrying our wedding photo, Mitch in jeans, me with a flower in my hair, the judge's desk as our background.

I held it up to him and pointed at me. "Do you see that girl, Mitch? Do you really see her? Because I can tell you right now what she was thinking, what she wanted. She wanted you. She wanted kids.

She wanted a life with adventure and laughter and Jesus, if she could just talk you into it. But that's not the life that this girl got," I said, now pointing at myself. "So before you throw around the phrase 'Do whatever you want,' or talk about how I get my way all the time, I want you to think about the girl in this picture. I can tell you with 100 percent certainty that the life she has is not anything close to what she wanted." I placed the portrait in the front hall closet and when I returned to the living room just moments later, Mitch was already gone.

My shoulders slumped. *Jesus, I don't know how much longer I can do this. Why does this have to be so hard?* I didn't hear an answer.

"I'm never going to have a boyfriend, and I'm sure never going to get married," Macey said. I hear myself in my daughter's voice. I want to tell her it doesn't have to be this way. I want to tell her there are really good men in the world who love Jesus, who could love her so well. I want to tell her that though I've never felt it myself, I've seen it in other people's lives. I want to tell her that she can have hope, that she can have dreams. I want to tell her that she can want love. I hear my daughter's words, and they are now my own. She got these words from me. She got them from watching me, watching me cry, watching me yell, watching me lie in bed in the middle of the day.

Love did this to me. A man's love did this to me. (Or perhaps better put: a man's lack of love did this to me.) And Macey sees me and knows instinctively what she doesn't want for her life. She doesn't want to love a man. She doesn't want to want a man. And she absolutely does not want to need a man. She will be fine on her own. She will not make the same mistakes her mother made. She will not be told what to do, be yelled at, be controlled, be manipulated, be lied to, and be called names. Her mother may not have the strength to do anything about it, but she sure as hell is not going to choose the life her mother chose. It may mean loneliness. It may mean bitterness. It may mean a hardened heart. It may mean some sadness. But she'd rather take all of that and more than take the chance of landing in the

FIVE

life of her mother. She'd rather die than follow in my footsteps. She loves me, but she doesn't respect me, doesn't want to turn out like me. And I don't blame her.

SIX

A COUPLE OF YEARS AGO, THE police came to our house. I had designated the season as, "If you drink, you can't sleep in our bed with me." This was after "If you drink, just don't drink in front of me," but before, "If you drink, don't drive with the kids." Each of these rules lasted for three to six months, and the drinking would seem to stop. Then I'd find a hidden bottle of gin, I'd install a new rule, and we'd start the dance again.

One late night when Mitch was out (I assumed he was drinking), I took it upon myself to mount a hook-n-eye lock on our bedroom door. I figured this way, if he stumbled home drunk, forgetting my latest rule, the not-easy-to-open door would simply deter him, and he'd go sleep on the couch downstairs.

I had fallen into the early stages of sleep, cell phone in hand, when I heard his footsteps coming up the stairs. I sat up on the edge of my bed and waited. My breath was quick and shallow. I could see the shadows of his feet underneath the door. I watched the door knob turn and be pushed open a half inch. It took him a moment to register what was going on. I could see his one eye looking at me.

"Are you kidding me?" he slurred. "Open the damn door, Jules. This is my house. This is my bedroom."

"We can talk in the morning, Mitch. I'm going to sleep now," I said breathlessly, trying to sound carefree, hoping he couldn't hear the fear that I was trying to tamp down. He pushed on the door again.

SIX

"Jules, dammit, open the door!" Instinctively, I stood up, back to the door, and pushed against it. We pushed back and forth for perhaps a minute. I slid to the floor and used the leverage of the bed to push against. He was stronger than me, no doubt. But my adrenaline had kicked in. I had a point to make. A few days earlier he had told me, while sober, that I made him sick, that my neediness made him physically ill. The weight of my shame and pain from those words was giving me the strength to keep the door from caving in on me.

I remembered I had my phone. Greg had told me in passing a few months prior that if I ever needed anything, that if Mitch ever hurt me, I could call him, no matter the time. The embarrassment that would have kept me from calling him in the light of day was nowhere to be seen as I punched in his number.

"Greg, it's Jules. I've locked Mitch out of the bedroom, and he's trying to force his way in. And you said I could call you ..."

"I'm on my way," Greg responded. "Stay on the phone with me. Just keep talking."

I wanted Mitch to hear me. I wanted him to know that he had been told on, that someone knew what he was doing. He stopped pushing on the door. It was quiet for a few moments, then I heard him go downstairs.

I whispered, "I think he gave up. He just went downstairs."

"I'll still come over ... I'll feel better," Greg said.

"Okay. Thank you. This is so crazy. I feel like an idiot, calling you." I began moving the dresser to block the door.

Footsteps.

"He's coming back up."

"Stay on the line, Jules."

I leaned against the side of the bed, legs extended, trying to secure the door against Mitch. He slipped a knife between the door and door jam. *Didn't I see this in a movie once? How is this actually happening to me?*

"What's going on, Jules? Talk to me."

"He's got a knife."

"I'm going to hang up and call the police. I'm almost there. I will call you right back."

I watched as the knife slid up then connected with the hook as he pushed it upward to unlatch it. I could no longer hold the door shut. It flew open, Mitch behind it, pushing me onto the bed. I jumped up and ran past him but not before smelling the stench of his evening's bad choices.

I ran downstairs to our living room, not wanting to run out of the house and leave Mitch alone with our kids. I positioned myself with my back to our front window and my body facing the stairs. I went to flip on the light but it didn't turn on. I looked across to the dining room and the clock was blank. Had he cut off the power?

Greg called back and I answered immediately, "I'm downstairs now, but I'm not leaving him in the house with Macey and Jordan."

"The police are on their way," Greg said.

Mitch came back down the stairs and walked toward me. I recounted his every move to Greg, hoping this would dissuade him. It didn't. We were separated by our couch, and he began to pace back and forth.

"Are you happy now?" he taunted. "Are you talking to Lauren? What's she going to do? Tell her I said hi." There would be moments of long, dark silence as he stared at me. And then he'd start up again. "If you had just let me come up to my bed, this never would've happened. The kids heard everything, by the way. Hope you're proud of yourself." He straightened up and walked back upstairs.

"He went upstairs," I whispered into the phone.

"Okay, sit down for a minute," said Greg. "Take a breath."

I could hear furniture moving, hear Mitch grunting. He must've been putting the room back together. He came back down and tossed the hook-n-eye on the couch between us. "Did you actually think that little thing would stop me?" he laughed.

Red and blue lights bounced off our walls. "You can't be serious. You called the police?" As I ran out of the house, I saw him turn. I was sure he'd follow me out to tell the cops what a fool I was, but he didn't. Greg met me in the driveway as an officer stepped out of his car.

SIX

"What's going on here, Ma'am?"

"I didn't call you, my friend did. My husband has been drinking, and he tried to come into our room even though I locked the door. He used a knife to get in." Being in shock, I was speaking fast and loud and, I'm sure, making no sense.

"Ma'am, did he hurt you?"

"Well, no, but …"

"Why didn't *you* call?"

"I've never done this before … I …"

"What do you want us to do for you, Ma'am?"

"I want you to get my husband out."

"Is his name on the title?"

"What?"

"Is his name on the title to the house?"

"Well, yes, but …"

"Then he has every right to be here. In fact, and I'll tell your husband this too, if this had been me, and my wife had locked me out of any room of the house, I would have broken the door down. You can't lock your husband out of his house or out of a room in his house."

"I just wanted to sleep … I just wanted to feel safe." My mind switched, "My kids are in there with him." The officer called to his partner and told him to go in. As I stood in the front yard, I saw the officer walk into our darkened house, flashlight on. Mitch was hiding in the bathroom. The officer convinced him to come out and they talked on the front steps for a few minutes.

The officers then switched, getting both of our sides of the story again. "You lucked out. If you had broken his nose or caught his fingers in the door while pushing back and forth, I'd be taking you away for aggravated assault right now."

"I lucked out." I whispered, with a small laugh.

Both officers were now standing in front of me. One said, "Ma'am, it's obvious he's been drinking, but I think it's safe for all of you to spend the night here tonight."

"*What?* No. I won't."

"Well, we have no grounds to make him leave."

"Am I free to take my kids and go somewhere for the night?"

"Yes, that's well within your rights."

"Will you help me get them?" To Greg, "Will you call Lauren for me and tell her the kids and I are on our way?"

One of the officers walked with me around to the back of the house. The lights were still out. I was shaking, in my tank top and shorts. Seriously, this was an episode of *Cops*, starring me. When we got to Macey's room, she was rocking on her bed, all thirteen years of her. When she saw me, she started to cry. I wanted to hold her but I couldn't. As if a business transaction, I said to her, "Macey, I need you to pack a bag with some things. We're going to stay at Lauren's tonight."

We went across the hall to Jordan's room. He was asleep, at nine years old. Bless his heart. The tears came at this point. I was waking my son up with a police officer standing behind me. He would be terrified. I grabbed his backpack and filled it with some clothes. I leaned down by his bed. "Jordan," I whispered. "Jordan, I need you to get up. I'm so sorry, Honey. Everything's okay but I need you to get up. We're going to Aunt Lauren's house for the night. Come on, Honey." He opened his eyes and sat up, still mostly asleep. He stood up, saw the officer and looked at me, a face full of questions, but not saying one word. I handed him has backpack and the three of us were escorted back through our house. Greg put the kids in the car.

The officer handed me a piece of paper. "You probably won't be able to get an order of protection, but if you want to try for it, this is the procedure."

"Thanks." I didn't mean it.

As I got in the car, I saw Mitch. He was joking with one of the officers. He caught my eye, looked at me and smiled as if he had just won something. He kind of had.

SEVEN

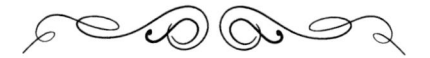

AFTER THE ARGUMENT OVER WHAT to tell the kids, I just had to get out of town. The kids stayed with my father and Lauren stepped in, once again, to save the day.

Lauren and I met in junior high. We were assigned to be lab partners in science, against both our wishes, we confessed to each other years later. I thought she was too pretty to do me any good, and she thought I was too smart and would make her feel stupid. Thirty years later, we both think the other is pretty *and* smart, and she's been the most constant person in my life to date. And, in my entire life, she's the only person I have led to Jesus, a banner moment in our early friendship.

So when she suggested that we get away for a few days, that maybe some time at her folks' cabins in Iowa might do us both some good, I jumped at the chance. And what a gift it was. The plan was to each do whatever we needed to do with God during the day, in solitude, and then meet up for dinner each night. We're the kind of friends that can allow the other the space we need. And it turns out, it was just what my heart needed.

The first day was jagged, uncomfortable, like I couldn't find myself in the midst of the quiet. I had taken a couple walks, read through my journal from the past few months, even brought along a few of my mom's letters. But something wasn't quite clicking for me. I had longed for this time away. Okay, my soul needed this time away. Yet, I felt stuck. I was all closed up deep down inside.

> God, I've been here a full day, and I've literally only said hi to you. I wonder why. I'm not far from you by any means. I've been spending time with you every morning like clockwork for a while now. I'm pretty weary, and I guess I could use some healing, but I would think that would've driven me straight into your arms, not hold you at arm's length.
>
> Unless ... unless I've become convinced that you haven't come through for me, are not coming through me, and therefore will never be coming through for me, so why bother? Why hope? Why talk to you?
>
> This feels like way too familiar territory, though. I already know that our definitions of "rescue" differ. That lesson was learned with my mom's death, with my miscarriage. You've never promised to swoop in and change all of my difficult circumstances. I get that. I had gotten to the place of grappling with your sovereignty and had come to accept the dichotomy that you are simultaneously good and loving all the while able, capable, and allowed to do whatever you want to those you love (i.e. me), and that you could because you are God and no one else is; but that when these horrible things happen, you "rescue" by providing unexplainable peace and strength to those who ask.

Ahhh, I think I'd stumbled onto something. I hadn't been feeling that peace and strength. I needed it. I had been begging for it. I was crawling through my life and not sustained in the least, not having enough emotional strength to even get through one full day it seemed. I had to admit that I simply wasn't feeling *God*. And that was leaving me alone to fight with my vain imaginations that God had up and left me to get through this thing, this life of mine, all on my own. Had he left me too?

After a nap, I pulled out the letters from Mom. My sixth and seventh years were well documented. Apparently I was quite the high achiever in first and second grade. But here's what Mom had to say when I was eight.

> Julianne, I'm having a hard time these days. I'm sad a lot. Your father and I are arguing more and again, I have to tell you how sorry I am that you are growing up in this. I'm hoping that not too much damage is being done. But I want to share a verse with you that has come to mean so much to me in my darkness lately. "I am going to lure her and lead her out into the desert; there, I will speak to her heart" (Hosea 2:14 ISV). God is leading me even in the dark times. And he will do that for you, too, my darling.

Tears hung on the brim of my eyes as I read and reread that verse. I went on to write in my journal ...

> I just realized that I've been lured and led all these years, just like you led my mother.
> Then I felt you say to me: *I am here. I am with you. I am holding you. I have heard every prayer and seen every tear you've cried. And I'm not letting go. I'm not letting go of you. I'm not letting go of Mitch. I'm not letting go of Macey and Jordan. Even when it doesn't seem like it, I am holding onto each of you. I am holding on to you, Beloved.*
> Oh Lord, my soul desperately needed these words. Is there anything you want me to know or do, Lord, before I head home?

SEVEN

> *You're carrying the weight of the world on your shoulders. You're trying to be strong. You're trying to hold your family together. And you're unhappy and lonely. So no, no new marching orders this time. I just want to remind you that I love you and I'm here. Let me be your Strength. Let me satisfy your ache.*

Thank you for meeting me here, Father.

─────✦─────

We sat on the porch swing of the cabin, letting the sounds of the summer evening wash over us for a while.

Finally I said, "My heart is growling."

"What are you talking about?" Lauren asked with a smile.

"You know how when you're hungry, your stomach growls?" I asked back.

"Yeah?" she answered.

"Well, it's my *heart* that's growling. It's starving," I said.

"Oh …" she said, her voice trailing off to a whisper.

And then we went back to swinging in silence, watching the sun go down, and letting the crickets fill up the quiet.

─────✦─────

Now home from the retreat, the kids were at school and Mitch was … well, not here. I don't know where exactly but that was becoming commonplace. Though I love the quiet of having the house to myself, today it felt too quiet for some reason. I'm in between events, no plans for the day, so I found myself wandering through my home, room to room. I'd stand in the doorway and look around as if seeing it for the first time. Walk in, pick up a knickknack, and examine a photo. When I got to Macey's room, I sat on her window seat and looked out over our backyard. This had been Macey's view her entire life. I realized that she could see into the detached garage from here. The window just above Mitch's workbench was in plain sight. If I could count the number of times I'd walked by her room or brought in laundry and found her sitting in this exact spot, with a book or her journal.

Her journal ... peeking out from under one of the pillows on the window seat. *I shouldn't look at it. If I were her age, I would not have wanted my mom to look at mine,* I argued with myself. *But she doesn't always tell me what's on her mind. But she's seventeen,* I sparred back.

This is ridiculous; I'm her mother. I need to know how she's doing, I convinced myself, picking it up and gently opening it to where the bookmark rested.

> I can see Daddy. How does he not know, after all these years, that I can see right in to his work shop? I don't know why he tells Mom that he's not drinking when I see him with a beer in his hand almost every time he's out there. Does he have to drink to be around us? To be around me? Am I that difficult to live with? This is where Jordan would say, "Duh, yeah ..."
>
> And why does Mom cover for him? She says she hates secrets, but she's keeping his. Is she doing it to protect him? Us? Herself?
>
> And Mom's been humming this song lately. I don't even think she realizes how often she's doing it. I asked her about it once and she said it was by someone named Carole King ... something about it being too late. So depressing.
>
> Tara's parents' divorce is on my mind lately. According to Tara's descriptions, her parents' marriage is romantic comedy compared to mine. So, does that mean it's only a matter of time? I hate this! I love my mom, I love my dad, (Jordan's okay), but I hate my family. I hate the fighting. I hate the lies. I hate the things that we can't talk about. I hate not knowing, not feeling secure. I used to feel secure, but not anymore. Everything feels upside down and like it could break open at any minute. And Jordan's off, doing his own thing, getting into trouble, which means I need to be as perfect as I can be. Jesus, will you help me with that?
>
> Well, that's all I've got for now.

SEVEN

Oh, Macey. I'm sorry, I'm sorry, I'm sorry, I'm sorry. I'm recreating my childhood in yours. I never wanted this life for you. Please forgive me, honey. I brushed a tear from my cheek. *Please forgive me, Jesus.* I tucked the journal back under the pillow where I found it and lie on her bed until the tears lulled me to sleep.

I ran into an old friend from college a while back. We were Christmas-card-only friends now. But she had known Mitch before I had known Mitch, and she asked me pointblank, "How are you still married to him?"

My eyes widened. How do you answer a question like this at all, let alone to someone you don't even know anymore? "What do you mean?" I asked. "We're fine. Mitch is great," I lied. There I go, lying again, master of subterfuge that I'm becoming.

"Jules, come on," she said. "Everyone knows that after he got his heart broken by Emily he just went through one girl after another, almost with a vendetta."

"We're fine. I need to go," I told her, quickly walking away.

So I'm part of a vendetta, huh? That would explain some things. But really, how am I still married to him? If there weren't a God and a vow and a Macey and a Jordan and a church community counting on me not to mess up and a watching world and a generational line coming up behind me, I'd walk away. But there are. There are all of these things and more. I've been created to be a reflector and, right now, if I walk away, I wouldn't be able to live with myself. I don't think.

EIGHT

"Mitch, do you understand why we're here today?" Dr. Grant asked. He sat across from us in his too-bright office. Mitch and I were forced to share a loveseat. Ironic. The lit fireplace was an unexpected touch but couldn't break through the chill I was trying to shake.

"Yes," he said. "It's a mandatory psychiatric evaluation required by the court," Mitch answered robotically, shifting in his chair.

Dr. Grant opened up a folder with several pages already in it, even though this was our first visit. *I'd pretty much give anything to see what was already written in there*, I thought to myself with a smirk.

"That's right," he said, "and as I can see you've opted to make it a couples' session, we might as well make the best of it," the doctor added encouragingly. I swear I saw Mitch roll his eyes like a twelve-year-old, but I could just be making that up.

"Since we have a few required sessions ahead of us to work through some of the main concerns, why don't you tell me if you want to start talking about your childhood, your life and family now, or the work-related situation that brought you here," he addressed Mitch.

"You decide," Mitch said unwillingly.

"Mitch, you said you'd keep an open mind," I chided him. I immediately regretted speaking up when he shot me a look of disdain. "Sorry," I whispered, looking down at my hands in my lap. I couldn't stop fidgeting with the tassel of my scarf.

EIGHT

"Well, okay," Dr. Grant said, "why don't we talk about how things are going in your life right now then?"

"Fine," Mitch said.

"Mitch, why don't you start by telling me about your family?" Dr. Grant asked.

Mitch looked out the window behind the doctor's desk. I followed his glance to a Budweiser truck trying to park on the street right outside the office. I couldn't help but wonder if he were wishing he could hijack that truck right about now. *Jules, watch it. Be nice.*

"Well, you've met Jules. We've been married about twenty years."

"Twenty-two," I corrected.

He continued, ignoring me. "We've got two kids. Macey's a senior in high school and our son, Jordan, is a sophomore. Jules runs an organization that puts together events for charities. And you know my current employment situation," Mitch finished with a forced laugh.

"Alright, good. How are you feeling about your current employment situation?" the doctor asked him.

"Well, I'm not a huge fan of not having a job," he answered quickly.

"Why not?" Dr. Grant pursued.

"Why not? Hmmm, let's see. I'm not able to provide for my family. I feel like a failure. I feel like I don't have a purpose. I feel like I let my co-workers down. I feel like I'm letting everybody down, come to think of it," he said. "Take your pick," he finished.

I turned to look at him. Though it was only about four sentences, this was the most I had heard him share about his situation. Up til this point, how he'd been feeling about everything that was going on had been pure conjecture on my part.

"Mitch, I didn't know you were feeling all those things," I said, touching his arm.

He moved his arm so my hand would fall away. "You've never asked," he answered icily.

I sighed deeply and turned back to face the doctor. "Would you say that's an accurate statement, Jules?" the doctor asked me.

"Well, I don't ask him every day how he's doing or feeling, but I know I've asked him a couple times. Besides, I haven't wanted to bug him a lot because I figured this was a sensitive subject and thought he might feel like I were rubbing it in or nagging. I didn't realize it was coming across to him as a lack of concern," I said.

"Mitch, does what Jules just said make sense to you?" he asked.

"Sure, but that's just the tip of the iceberg. And I'm not going there today," he said.

I felt my shoulders tense and noticed that the scarf tassel was wrapped so tightly around one of my fingers that the circulation was starting to cut off. I fidgeted some more to undo it and closed my eyes for a moment, taking in slow breaths.

Living with Mitch has done so much damage to my psyche. Not just his drinking, but his continual lying that leads me to constantly question my own perceptions. And the correcting and questioning that leads me to constantly look at myself as an idiot who, only by the grace of God, could make it through the day on her own. I repeat mantras like *I am precious and honored in your sight* and *you love me even though Mitch doesn't* to get through argument after argument, trying to convince myself of my worth. I finally know these things to be truth. I am so grateful that for whatever reason, these days, I am turning to God more and more as my mirror, not Mitch, to find out who I really am.

"Jules, what are you thinking right now?" Dr. Grant asked me.

"I'm thinking this is Mitch's session so he can talk about whatever he wants. And I'm thinking that he's right. There is an iceberg and we never talk about it, and I don't know if I have the energy to do so anyway," I answered, my voice filled with resignation. There are no allowances in our fragile relationship for me to heal out loud. I should be healed already. Or worse yet, Mitch might actually believe there is nothing for me to heal from.

My cell phone rang, startling us all. "I'm sorry, I thought I put it on silent," I said, looking down to check the number. It was the high school. "Would you excuse me? I need to take this," I said, and got up and left the room.

"Hello?" I answered.

EIGHT

"Mrs. Millhouse, this is Principal Lawson over at the high school," he said.

"Yes. How can I help you?" I replied, noticing my forehead was getting warm.

"I needed to check in with you because Jordan has had four unexcused absences in the past two weeks, and today was the fifth, so our policy is to call home," he said.

"You mean he's not at school right now?" I asked.

"I'm afraid not. And it sounds like this is news to you, as well," he commented.

"Yes, it is. I've had no idea that he's been skipping. Thank you for calling. We'll talk to him when he comes home today," I said, pacing quickly up and down the hallway.

"That's fine, but you need to know that he's got a week of detention for every day he's skipped. That needs to be explained to him clearly, because he hasn't been serving them, and I don't think he understands that suspension is the next level of consequence," Mr. Lawson stated.

"Alright. I'll make sure he understands. I'm so sorry about this. And thank you, again, for calling," I said, hanging up. *What's one more thing*, I thought to myself.

I walked back into the office to see Mitch standing up in disgust. He brushed past me and muttered, "I'll be in the car."

"What just happened?" I asked Dr. Grant, confused.

"Sometimes people are surprised to hear what comes out of their own mouths, and then they have to blame it on someone else. And that's usually me," he replied. "It's okay, I've seen this before," he continued.

"Can you tell me what he said?" I asked him.

"Why don't you ask him yourself?" the doctor suggested. I gave him a look as if to say, *you've met my husband, right?*

"I'll see you the same time next week," he said to me as I grabbed my purse.

"Yes," I answered, pretty much assuming I'd never see the guy again if Mitch had his way. "It was nice to meet you," shaking his hand and turning to leave. I reached the doorway and turned around. "Do you think this would help us?" I asked him. "Coming to see you, I mean?"

"That depends on Mitch more than any of us," he answered prophetically.

That's what I was afraid of, I thought to myself, forcing a smile and walking out.

~~~

"We need to show a united front to Jordan," I said to Mitch as we walked into the house after I explained the whole situation in the car on the way home. "He should be home any minute, and we don't have a plan," I said.

"I think we should ground him, and I think we should drive him to and from school to make sure he's going," Mitch said. He grabbed the back of his neck and started rubbing. He looked tired.

"Headache?" I asked him.

"Not really," he said, dropping his hand.

"Okay, I agree on the driving. That's fine, and there should be a consequence. But I think the detentions are consequence enough for skipping school. I'm more concerned about his heart and what's really going on here," I said.

"What's going on here is that we have a rebellious fifteen-year-old on our hands who thinks he can get away with stuff," Mitch replied.

"I think it's bigger than that," I said quietly.

"What do you mean?" Mitch asked.

"It's no secret that our life these days is a bit out of whack and the kids are feeling it. I think this might be Jordan's way of trying to get our attention, get through to us maybe," I answered quietly.

"I think you're making this bigger and deeper than it really is, which you do a lot by the way," Mitch said.

Does every freaking thing have to be about our relationship? I wanted to shout. It's little moments like this when I realize, again, that Mitch is my nemesis in so many ways.

"I've got some things to do. Can you handle this with Jordan?" he asked.

EIGHT

Defeated, "Sure," I responded. "I'll take care of it." *I always take care of it. You know, sometimes I just give up. I really do. I know, Lord, that you "lovingly" decided this would be my hard thing in life, but today I hate my hard thing.*

Mitch left the room just as the bus pulled up. I watched Jordan walk up our driveway. *When did he grow up? When did I lose him?* I saw him stop, reach in his backpack and pull out a piece of gum. *He hates gum*, I thought. He walked in the back door and looked surprised to see me standing in the kitchen. "Hey, Mom," he said, walking past me quickly, not making eye contact.

"Hey, Hon, do you have a few minutes? I'd like to talk to you about something," I said, sitting down at the kitchen table.

"Umm, not really," he said, standing in the doorway. "Got a lot of homework," he said as he turned to walk away.

"Jordan, come here. We need to talk," I said more firmly than either of us had been used to. I'm realizing that I've been letting Macey and Jordan walk all over me as I try to balance out Mitch's harshness. Turns out, it doesn't work that way.

Surprised again, he came back, put his backpack on the floor, and sat down at the table.

Lord, some wisdom please. "Before I start talking, is there anything you want to tell me?" I asked him.

He looked down. "What do you mean?" he asked.

"I mean, is there anything going on in your life that you might want to share with me? And let me remind you what I've been saying for years, things will always get back to me one way or another," I said.

"I maybe skipped school last week," he answered.

"Maybe?" I asked.

"Okay, I did," he answered sharply.

"And just last week?" I asked, again.

"No," he said.

"How often, Jordan?" I asked.

"Today was maybe my fourth or fifth time," he answered.

"Today wasn't *maybe* your fourth or fifth time, today *was* your fifth time. The school called," I said. "What's going on, Jordan?" I asked.

"Nothing. I just hate school," he said.

"I don't buy it," I said. "You've never loved school, but you've never even considered skipping until recently. Talk to me," I persuaded.

Then I noticed something. His eyes were a little glassy. *God, please no … not Jordan too.*

"I hate school, and I hate home, okay? So I meet Drew at the park and we hang out. That's all there is to it!" he yelled. "Now just leave me alone about it," he said, standing up. He tripped on his backpack, kicked it, and walked out of the kitchen.

"Jordan," I said, following him. "Jordan, get back here." With that, I heard his bedroom door slam. I went back to the kitchen and noticed his open backpack. I walked over and picked it up, instantly feeling guilty. I looked inside anyway. *What was I supposed to do?* A couple notebooks. A textbook. Pack of gum. A five dollar bill. Something crinkly, a pack of cigarettes. My shoulders slumped. *Nooo.* Then my ring clinked against something. I pulled out a mini bottle of gin like you'd find on a plane. It was empty. *Oh Lord, why my sweet boy?* I started to cry and slipped down into a chair.

Jordan walked back in to find me clutching the small bottle with his backpack open at my feet. "Who said you could go through my stuff?" he yelled, grabbing the backpack. "I can't believe you did that, Mom!" He walked out the back door, slamming it, and walked down the driveway as I lay my head on the table and cried.

Mitch walked back in to the kitchen. "How'd it go?" he asked casually, leafing through the mail on the counter, without looking at me.

"Well, I found cigarettes and a small bottle of gin in Jordan's backpack," I said icily, standing up and walking toward him. "I wonder where he picked up those great habits," I sneered, slamming both on the counter next to Mitch. I didn't wait for a response before picking up my car keys and heading out the door.

I drove to the park just minutes from our house. It's become my oasis when I just can't breathe at home. I've taken to leaving my mom's letters in my glove compartment, along with a small Bible for moments just like this. I've had enough of these kinds of moments by

EIGHT

now that I've begun preparing for them like a flat tire. You just never know when you'll need some emotional reserves.

I parked, grabbed my things, and walked over to the bench by the stream. *My bench*, I thought and smiled. I rolled my neck a few times, closed my eyes, and took a few deep breaths. My hand fell to my side, resting on the bench. I was reaching for an invisible hand, but there was no one to hold it. No one had held my hand in probably a year.

God, everything is falling apart around me. I'm sorry for what I said to Mitch just now. Lord, I just really need your help here. Please speak to me, I prayed, and then opened up my Bible. Psalm 31:24 called out to me. It was as if God were speaking directly to my heart: *Be brave. Be strong. Don't give up. Expect me to get there soon.*

Oh Lord, I'm trying. But life is so hard right now. I feel alone. I am exhausted. I don't know what to do. About Mitch. About Jordan. About any of it. I promise not to give up. But please, please get here soon. Though I have to admit, I don't think I'm expecting it anymore. I'm sorry for my lack of faith.

I put my Bible down and watched two ducks in the stream. One, the female, had climbed out and was standing on the water's edge squawking at her mate. He just swam away like he didn't have a care in the world. *Just like at my house*, I thought with a small smile.

My mom's letters lay next to my Bible. I picked up the next one, opened the envelope, and pulled it out. The handwriting was different, smaller. It was my father's.

> Jules,
>
> I know your mother typically writes you a letter on your birthday, but she's not feeling up to par today, so she asked me to write a few words to you. You are double digits this year and I only know that because it's all you've been talking about for a month now.
>
> You are a lovely girl. You enjoy school and have a few good friends, but you prefer to be at home, in your room, on your bed with a book or a journal. Sounds a lot like me, come to think of it.

We've had a difficult year as a family, I'm afraid, and you are sensing it. You are spending even more time in your room these days and your mother is worried about you. I keep telling her you're a tough girl and you're just fine, but she worries. I do want to say, though, that I am sorry for the arguing. I know it's gotten worse as you've gotten older, and I take the blame for that. But we both love you, even when you might not think we do. Or even when you might not think we love each other.

Alright, not sure what else your mother would want me to say, so I'll stop now. Happy birthday, double-digit girl.

Love, Dad

I realized I had been holding my breath and took in a deep gulp of air. Though my father was a writer by trade, he rarely, if ever, expressed himself that way to me. Reading his words was a healing balm and brought me some hope.

People make mistakes. They feel badly about them. Families go through difficult times. Though I knew mine currently was, and my family of origin had, it was good to hear that sometimes it's just part of life and you just make it through.

Thank you, Jesus. These words today, your words and my dad's words, have given me some strength already. I may not know what I'm going to do about Jordan or Mitch today, but I know that you are here for me. And I know that I can do whatever it is you need me to do. Thank you for meeting me here. I need you.

With that, I picked up my Bible and the letters, took another look at the squabbling ducks, and headed back to the car, feeling a bit more ready for what was waiting for me when I got home, whatever that might be.

As I reached the car, I looked up across the park and saw Jordan and a friend leaning against the swing set. I saw his friend nod toward me and Jordan look over my way. I smiled a small smile and put my hand up in a half wave. He seemed to say goodbye to his friend, and

EIGHT

started walking toward me. I tossed my stuff in the car and began walking to meet him halfway.

Jordan and I have had a special connection since he was about six weeks old. It didn't come immediately for me like it did with Macey. In fact, I feared it wasn't going to come at all. I hadn't known what to do with a boy. But then something just clicked and I knew he'd have my heart for the rest of my life. When he was about two, I wrote in my journal that I knew I should eat up all of the sweet moments of him following me around and loving me like I was the best thing on earth, because I knew that at any moment that could stop. Then one time when we were on an airplane when he was about ten, he reached his hand over to my cheek and stroked it. I couldn't believe that he still thought I hung the moon. Looking back, that was the last time he affirmed me so publicly. And now ... well, now it's like he moved out and someone else moved in. And my heart can hardly stand it. I miss my son and he's standing right in front of me.

When we were a few feet apart, we both stopped, and I said, "I'm sorry I looked in your backpack."

"I'm sorry I yelled at you," he responded quietly, showing me just a bit of the true heart of my little boy.

"You've got to let me in, Honey. Do you have any idea how much I love you? How much I worry about you?" I asked him. "Please don't push me away. Please tell me what's going on with you," I pleaded.

"School's harder this year than I thought. And ..." he started, then paused, thinking. "And things seem bad at home. You and Dad are fighting more. Something's going on with his job that no one's talking about. And I know he's drinking. That bottle you found in my backpack, I found it in his stash in the basement," he said, looking at the ground. A tear slipped down his face and landed on his shoe.

"Oh, Honey," I said, walking toward him, pulling him into my arms. He might be taller than I am, but he was still my baby. "I'm so sorry about all of these things. Our life is crazy right now, I know, and I'm sorry it's hurting you so much," I whispered. "But I am so, so glad that we are talking about it all, because now we can actually deal with it," I said.

I pulled away. "Oh my word, is your friend still here?" thinking he might be embarrassed to be seen hugging his mother.

"It's okay," Jordan said and hugged me again.

"We'll figure this whole thing out together, okay? I promise," I said, putting my arm through his as we started to walk back to the car. "Jesus will help us work this whole thing out," I said, more as a prayer than a knowing.

NINE

Jesus, the more I do it, the easier it gets. At least, this is what I keep telling myself. It's funny— or sad, depending on how you look at it—how I can barely stand the sight of Mitch anymore, and yet I am able to turn off my every thought and feeling to have sex. Though I draw the line at "sex while drunk," any other time is fine. It has nothing to do with him. I think of something else. I think of someone else. (I know, I know. I'm sorry.) I sometimes think about nothing at all.

His touches are rough and disconnected. He doesn't know, after all these years, what I like and don't like. But it's not even about that anymore. I am doing what I am supposed to be doing as his wife, what all the Christian marriage books tell me to do time and again as if it's some kind of supernatural elixir that will win him back. As if it will make him chose me over gin. It never once has. If given a choice, he will always choose that bottle. So I do what I am told. I let him do whatever he wants to me and sometimes, I actually enjoy it. It's just sex, nothing else. I'm sometimes almost surprised not to find some money on my nightstand. This is not an act of love between us. We have never in all of our sexual encounters looked each other in the eyes. He tells me that he loves me, but only during,

NINE

in the heat of the moment. This is how he shows me that he loves me, his version of showing, his version of love. It makes me sick to think about it: how desperate I am for any kind of touch and affection, that I will take that, that sometimes I even want it. It's even more heartbreaking that for a short while, I thought that was how it was supposed to be. In my marriage, I've never known a kiss or a touch from a man who knows me, and loves me, and I suspect I never will.

There was one time—I'm guessing you remember this, God—deep into the marriage and all its horrors, when our counselor suggested we lean on each other, physically and emotionally. I was trying to do the right thing, and I asked Mitch if he wanted to have sex. His response, "Give me a minute, I'll have to divorce myself emotionally from the situation." A little part of my heart fell deeper into my chest cavity and never came back up. We had sex. But that was the last time for almost a year. When I told our counselor about it at our next appointment, he shook his head and said, "I'm so sorry, Jules ... That's not at all what I intended." So, for a while there, the more I did it, the easier it got. And then, I just stopped doing it. And now I just don't care.

***

When we were in high school, Steven and I would occasionally go out to eat at the local café. We would watch, and go on to make fun of, the older, married couples without anything to say. But deep down, I ached for them. The worst loneliness, I thought back then, must be the married-singles kind of lonely. How those couples would look only at their food, or around the room, or just past the shoulder of their spouse, but not directly at them. Steven and I promised that would never be us.

And then, two decades went by and I was the one sitting in the restaurant, stirring my soup longer than necessary to fill the silence between Mitch and me. And then we moved beyond that stage, we don't bother going to restaurants anymore. We don't bother doing a lot of things together anymore.

"Hey, Mitch," I said as I came around the corner, "We need to leave for the event in about an hour. I should get there a bit early to make sure everything's all set. This is one of my top clients." I was looking through some paperwork on the counter and continued, "I ironed your shirt and had your suit dry cleaned. You pretty much just need to pick out a tie and you're all set," I said, my exhaustion weighing down each word.

"Thanks, Babe!" Mitch said over enthusiastically, and walked out of the room quickly, not making eye contact.

I stood there looking at where Mitch had been standing when I came in. I walked over to the cupboard and opened it, finding the bottle of gin front and center. I pulled it out and looked at the label. Yesterday, I had marked the top of the label with a sharpie. Now, only one day later, it was already three quarters gone.

"You've got to be kidding me," I said out loud to no one. "I am not going to this thing with an inebriated husband! I'm in charge of it, and he'll make me look like a fool!" I sat down at the table and sighed. "*I* could use a drink," I said with a half-smile, still talking to myself. *What am I going to do?* I prayed. "I hate this," I said as I picked up my cell. "I absolutely hate this."

"Lauren? Hey, Hon, Mitch is toasted again. Can I use you as an excuse for him not coming with me tonight to my thing? Something like I decided at the last minute that tonight was going to be more work than I thought, and so I'm bringing you with me instead?" I paused, listened.

"That would be great; I don't want to be a liar. Okay, thank you, Honey. I could use your company tonight anyway. Okay, I'll pick you up about five. Thank you so much, this means a lot to me."

NINE

"Mitch?" I said, walking back into the bedroom. "Don't worry about the tie, after all. Turns out this event is probably going to be more complicated than I thought, so Lauren is going to come work it with me. That means you get a free pass tonight," I said, giving him a hopefully convincing smile. I took in a quick breath and braced for Mitch's response.

Mitch's eyes narrowed as he stared at me. "The event is going to be *complicated*?" he accused. His shoulders tensed as he ripped the tie off from around his neck and threw it on the bed. He walked toward me, and I shifted slowly from foot to foot. "Just tell me the truth. You don't want to go with *me*," he said loudly.

"Mitch, I don't want to fight. I'm sorry for cancelling on you at the last minute. I appreciate your willingness to go with me in the first place," I explained. "Besides, I thought you'd be relieved," I continued, "I know how you hate these things."

"What's the real reason, Jules?" he asked, leaning on the dresser, within inches of my face. I winced when I caught a whiff of gin on his breath.

I stood my ground. "You've been drinking today. I'm not going to discuss this any further right now. I've made up my mind, and I need to get ready now," I said as I walked into the bathroom, closing the door behind me.

When he heard the click of the lock, Mitch turned, picked up a bottle of his cologne and threw it against the door, missing it by several inches. He grabbed his keys and stormed out.

I started my ritual: pulling out a CD and fast forwarding to my new mantra.

> It has been awhile, since I've seen another light besides the one I hold,
> Am I on my own ... all alone down here where it's becoming dark and cold
> So I ask, are you here with me ...
> ("I Will Go Before" by Justin Unger) [1]

I sat back down on the floor, tissue in hand, and hugged my legs to my chest. I rested my head on my knees and closed my eyes as the tears rolled down my cheeks. I sang softly along, stopping only to wipe a tear or raise my hand in prayer.

> Jesus, bring me your life in the middle of this mess. You alone know how tired I am. I can't keep doing this for another day, let alone another year. I lay this all down. I give you this great pain and my great need. Please enter in. And please give me the energy right now to get back up and do the things that you've placed in front of me to do. Help me focus on you and not on me so I can do my job tonight and do it well. Please replace my sadness with your joy. Surprise me with your goodness tonight. Please, Jesus. I need you.

I stood up, took a deep breath, wiped my face with a washcloth, and started to get ready for the event, the song repeating over and over in the background, renewing my soul as best as it could.

I'm shuffling through my regrets today like an iPod playlist going back twenty-five years. And if I could get that one day back, I wouldn't have told him that I loved him. I wouldn't have told him first. I would have waited to see if he would have said it to me. Here's the thing. I'm pretty sure he wouldn't have.

We had been all over the Florida coast that day, him visiting me while on assignment. We were fighting and getting along, back and forth all day. I couldn't stand to be with him some moments, couldn't breathe during others in the fear that I had pushed him too far with my neediness. We ended the night at the beach with a bottle of cheap strawberry wine, the only thing we could find. I told him that I hated that I didn't know, still, if he loved me. We sat staring at the ocean, me crying, basically begging him to tell me if he loved me.

He took forever to answer me. I hate that he took forever. I hate all his reasons for why he hadn't yet. They were practical and logical and I guess they made sense but it hurt. I wanted him more than he

NINE

wanted me. I loved him more than he loved me. I needed him more than he needed me.

I never wanted to be that girl. Everyone in my life was already like this. Meaning, I loved everyone else in my life more than they loved me. Not actions-love, but feelings-love. I feelings-loved everyone too much. More than they loved me back. The difference with Mitch is that I was outright telling him this. I was telling him how much I loved him. I was scaring the crap out of this twenty-three-year-old boy. He wasn't a man yet. He didn't know what it meant to love someone, neither did I really. But, I told him I did, and begged him to reciprocate.

So, he did. "I love you too," he said. "I do. I just wasn't going to say it for a while."

We got back to the hotel, and the needy little girl in me won an argument with the trying-to-be-grown-up girl in me. I said to him, too late at night to still be talking, "Do you really love me?"

He was worn out, worn down. I had broken him down. I'm sure he had visions of getting on the first plane in the morning and never looking back. I'm sure he had visions of me glomming on to him for the rest of our lives, walking around behind him, tugging on his shirtsleeve, *but do you love me, do you love me?* I scared him. I exhausted him. I didn't know what else to do.

As a girl, I'm convinced I was created to respond in a male/female relationship. But that has not been the role I have taken in our relationship, out of insecurity mainly. This is something I deeply regret. I went on to scare him, and exhaust him, and deplete him. I have initiated every step of our relationship, from first date to first kiss, to begging him to marry me, to babies, to counseling, to everything, all in the hopes that he'd realize he loved me after all. Every single thing I did over the past twenty years has been, basically, begging Mitch to love me. I was not created to have to beg for love. I was created to respond. I won't beg him to stop drinking. I won't beg him to be engaged in our life. And I most certainly will not beg him to love me anymore. Ever again.

"Thank you so much for being my plan B ... *again*," I said to Lauren as she slid into the passenger seat.

"My pleasure. I had nothing else going on, and you know how I love to dress up!" Lauren laughed. "So, how bad was it this time?"

"You mean, before I called you or after I told him he wasn't coming?"

"Both," Lauren answered with an empathetic smile.

"Well, he's going through bottles of gin like they're going out of style. I probably should just stop marking them but I can't seem to help myself. With so little control over this whole thing, I guess doing that makes me feel like I've got a bit of a handle on it. I can't stop him, but at least I can attempt to know how much he's drinking, can't I?" I asked.

"Unless ..." Lauren stopped herself.

"I know," I said. "Unless he's got bottles hidden in other places, and I'm just wasting my time, or worse yet, obsessing."

"Well, listen," Lauren said, "I don't know anything about this really, but I can't help but wonder if it's really just unhealthy for you to keep tabs on him like that. I don't know ..." she trailed off. "So, how did he take it when you said I was going instead of him?" she asked, changing subjects.

"Typical Mitch. In other words, not well. He yelled at me, he accused me of lying to him, and when I came out of the bathroom, I tripped on a bottle of cologne that he had apparently thrown at the bathroom door. So, you know, just a regular night at the Millhouse's," I said with another weary laugh. "I'm just so tired of this."

"I know, Hon. I'm so sorry," Lauren replied sympathetically. "You know what though? You can do this. You've *been* doing this. I know it's hard, but you are strong. And I know you're tired, but Jesus is helping you with this. You've told me that yourself."

"You're right, I know. I just really don't know how much more of this I can take," I sighed.

NINE

Father, I fully surrender to this trial: this so-far-twenty-five-year trial that will be a part of my life (sobriety or not) for the rest of my life. There is no getting out of it. I am here. This is my life. He is my appointed character-definer (and I humbly recognize that I am more than likely his). And this is my appointed circumstance to draw closer to you. So today, I embrace it. This surrender does not diminish my sadness or loneliness. This acceptance of my reality is not my way of saying it's all okay. I will never think this quasi-sin/disease-combo is okay. But I am committed to standing up to it and to breaking the cycle. Starting with me, recovery—not disease—will be passed down. And though it's a daily, uphill battle that will take all I've got and more, I'm not alone in the fight. And I will keep walking this hard road even if I never see the results in my lifetime.

TEN

I HAD BEEN HEADING OUT TO meet Lauren for dinner one night a few years back, waiting on Mitch to get home to stay with the kids. "I love you, Hon, but you've got to stop making me late," I said, with a laugh, when he finally showed up. I was actually detaching. I actually didn't care all that much that Mitch was late, therefore making me late. But what caught me by surprise was my flippant, "I love you." I meant it more as a phrase, a cliché. Because the last time I told Mitch that I loved him was in response to his profession during sex. And when the nausea welled up inside of me, I knew I no longer meant it, and could no longer say it. That was the last time I told my husband I loved him, three years ago. But I have a feeling I stopped meaning it years before.

"Hey, Mom, Dad just asked me to go out for ice cream. Wanna come?" Macey asked.

"No thanks, Hon," I said. But then my mind immediately shifted to Mitch's demeanor earlier today. He'd seemed off. "Mace, wait ..." I called, after she left the kitchen. I walked out to the living room only to see Mitch toss her the car keys nonchalantly as they headed out the door. *Thank You, Jesus, for this time. But will I ever be able to just let my kids do stuff with their dad without panic gripping my heart?*

TEN

I've been tiptoeing around this for years. Literally, years. My kids aren't dumb. They have both made mention of the problems in our family, of the drinking. And each time, I pat the proverbial elephant that lives in our house on the rump and walk around it. I think a huge part of me has thought somewhere deep down that if I don't actually say the words to my children, "Daddy has a drinking problem," that the problem would not exist. But denial and attempted authenticity make for strange bedfellows.

I'm a truth girl. I live on what's real. Maybe it's the reporter in me, I don't know. But I cannot stand thinking there is a reality running parallel to mine that I know nothing about, or worse yet, that has been hidden from me by lies.

My kids are teenagers. They have past the point of being tempted that first time, of being offered a cigarette or drink or drug, even in the cocoon I've tried to grow them up in. There's actually a good chance that I've waited too long to talk with them. But I can't go back in time and fix it. I can only take a look at what's right in front of me and deal with it head on. And what's right in front of me are a beautiful and amazing young woman and young man who need me to speak some words that they've been longing to hear. I need to put a name to the problem so that they can know in their hearts it's not because of them.

Will it hurt them to hear it? Yes. Will it hurt me to say it? Yes. Will it hurt Mitch to have his secret no longer kept? Yes. But, isn't the alternative even worse?

"Thank you so much for fitting me in today, Pastor Aaron," I said as I sat down in the chair across from the pastor's desk.

"Absolutely, Jules," he said, turning his computer monitor off and putting his cell phone on silent. "What can I do for my favorite charity event planner today?" he asked with an unsuspecting smile. "You're not here to hit me up for a donation, are you?" he laughed.

"Well, ummm ..." I stammered. My entire speech went out the window. Something about sitting right in front of my pastor made all my words just up and leave my head. "Okay ... well, I need some help," I forced out.

"Okay," he said slowly, nodding his head. "Hopefully you've come to the right place."

"I didn't know where else to turn. We just began counseling ..." I started, but Pastor Aaron interrupted.

"*We* meaning you and Mitch, I'm assuming?" he asked.

"Sorry. Yes, Mitch and I just started counseling ..." I continued.

"How is he doing, by the way? I know this whole losing a job thing must be difficult on him," he said, cutting me off again.

Frustrated but trying to appear unruffled, I said, "Well, that's sort of what I wanted to talk to you about. He didn't just lose his job, but that's a whole other story," I said, shifting in my chair. I felt I had to talk fast, without thinking first, because he kept interrupting me. I hated that about him. I mean, nice guy and everything, but *you're a pastor, let me finish a sentence, will ya?*

"Mitch has a drinking problem, and I don't know what to do about it," I blurted out. *Well, guess it's finally out there,* I thought. Lauren's known for years about Mitch, but no one else has. It wasn't as freeing as I thought it would be to say it out loud. "Oh, and I think Jordan might be getting himself into some trouble too," I said heavily.

"Oh," he said, surprised. "I didn't see that one coming," he said with an awkward laugh. "Mitch, huh?"

"Yep," I said quietly.

After thinking for a moment, he asked, "Is Mitch in a men's group?"

Is Mitch in a men's group? What does that have to do with anything? I yelled in my head. "No," I answered with a curt smile.

"Mm-hmm," he murmured, now looking in a desk drawer. He pulled out a brochure, then handed it to me across the desk. "This is a listing of all our small groups," he said, as if presenting me with a gift, a one-size-fits-all remedy.

"Alright," I said slowly, thinking, *got anything else back there?* "Not to sound selfish here, but I think *I* might need some help. I don't think *I'm* handling this very well. It's been going on for years and I just feel ..." *how should I put this?* "... trapped," I said, holding my breath.

TEN

"Let me start by saying that I've heard it floating around out there that there are the three A's of divorce: abuse, addiction, and adultery. But you need to know, Jules, that those are not biblical. You cannot leave because of a supposed addiction," he said. *Was that supposed to cheer me up?* I thought, anger flashing inside me. I just nodded and bit the inside of my cheek so I wouldn't say something I regretted. "May I ask you a couple questions?" he requested, leaning forward and folding his hands on his desk.

"Sure. I've got nothing to hide," I answered, looking him straight in the eyes. With that, Pastor Aaron seemed to become uncomfortable and leaned back in his chair, shifting his gaze.

"You've been married how long?" he asked.

"Twenty-two years," I answered, matter-of-factly.

"And how long would you say he's had a drinking problem?" he asked.

"I never really thought much of his drinking before we got married. I've only noticed it becoming a problem— and when I say *problem*, I mean that I think he drinks more than he should and he hides it from me—over the past twelve or fourteen years maybe," I said.

"Does Mitch think he has a problem?" he asked.

"You'd have to ask him," I said icily.

"Fair enough," he said. "When does he drink? What seem to be his triggers?" he asked.

"He definitely drinks after we fight, but it's gotten worse with his job situation. And any time he's stressed. But he seems to use just about anything as an excuse lately," I said.

"When you fight, huh?" he said. He raised his arms, placed his interlocked hands behind his head, and leaned back in his chair. "Is that something you can work on, you think?" he asked me. "You becoming less of a trigger for him?"

My eyes narrowed. Did my pastor just suggest that I am why Mitch drinks? That maybe if I were, you know, a bit nicer, a little less me, this wouldn't be such a problem? "Are you implying that Mitch drinks *because* of me?" I asked defensively.

"I'm just saying it might be something to look into," he said. He reached into another file on his desk and pulled out a list. Pastors and their magical lists. "These are the names of counselors that the church has approved. We've organized them based on their specialties," he said. As he handed me the list, he added, "You'll see there are three that specialize in anger management," he finished.

Oh, I'll show you anger management, I thought with a quick smirk. I took the list. I was hoping he wouldn't notice my hand shaking, thereby proving his hypothesis. *My pastor even thinks it's my fault. Mitch is right. If I weren't such a bitch, if I loved him better, and we didn't fight as much, he probably wouldn't drink.*

I stood up. I needed to get out of that office immediately. "Thank you for your time, Aaron," I said, purposely leaving *pastor* off. I took the small groups brochure and the anger management specialists list and turned to leave.

"Hey, Jules, are you still serving in Women's Ministry?"

I hesitated. "Yes," I said slowly. "I'm on the leadership team over one of the committees for events, why?"

"I'm going to need to talk this through with Cathryn, but I think you should step down for a while. You know, let some of the dust settle." He smiled.

Kicked in the gut, "I don't know what to say."

"Take some time to heal up …" he continued, as if clearing everything up. "Hey," he said, standing up, "what about Jordan?" he asked. "And at least let me pray for you three," he added, seemingly proud of himself for another job well done.

"I need to go, but feel free to pray for us when I leave," I answered, seething deep down inside. Thanks for nothing is what I wanted to say.

When I got in my car, I threw the brochure and the list on the floor of the passenger seat, gripped the wheel and began to sob. Maybe he really does drink because of me. Maybe I actually drive another human being to have to numb himself, just to be with me. Maybe I am the reason my marriage is falling apart and my life is a complete mess. *Oh, Jesus, I went for help and this is what I get? A couple lists, a finger*

TEN

pointed at me, and now I have to step down from ministry? Please give me wisdom. Please, please just heal me. I'm desperate.

You're not alone, I felt him whisper clearly.

I looked up and wiped the tears away. Remembering Mom's letters, I reached down to the now-familiar pile and pulled out the next few. It was the usual fare through my early teens but something grabbed my attention in my fourteenth year.

> I'm attending a support group, my darling, and it has made all the difference in the world to me. I hope you don't judge me or your father when I tell you this, but it's Al-Anon. Our marriage had been getting worse and your father's drinking seems to be progressing. Did you even know that your father drank? Well, I finally realized I needed help, and my dear Julianne, it has changed my life. The interesting thing is that your father still drinks and our relationship is still tenuous, but I am not as sad as I used to be, and we aren't fighting like we used to. It's not a magic pill or anything but it's bringing some peace to our family, finally.

Dad drank? How did I not see this? Or did I know deep down? Why did we never talk about this? And Mom went to Al-Anon? Isn't that group for people whose husbands beat them when they're drunk or crashed up their cars? But Mom said it was really helping.

Come to think of it, I remember the summer between junior high and high school noticing the fighting had all but stopped, and I just thought everything sort of got better on its own. When you're a kid, you don't really dissect your parents' relationship issues; you have no concept really what's going on behind the scenes. I had no idea. Al-Anon, huh?

<hr />

When I got home, there were grocery bags all over the counters. I sighed, ticked off that Mitch actually thought the groceries would put themselves away. I grabbed the first one, starting to pull items out. When my hand felt a cool, glass bottle neck, my heart stopped. I pulled out a bottle of gin. Then another. And then another. I dropped the bag on the floor and started crying. A fourth bottle smashed to the floor.

Mitch ran in, saw me crying, and immediately noticed the gin in my hand. He walked over to where I was standing, grabbed three of the bottles and walked back out the door getting into his car, and leaving me standing there in tears and shattered glass and spilled gin.

I was sitting on the front porch, reading awhile and trying to shake off my newest discoveries before the kids came home from school, when Greg pulled up in our driveway. *What's he doing here in the middle of the day?* He got out of his car and started walking toward me.

"Hey," he said.

"Hi," I replied, standing up before he could try to join me on the porch swing. He noticed and stopped himself from walking up the steps.

"Mitch isn't here," I said abruptly, looking around to see if any neighbors were outside.

"I know. I'm not looking for Mitch," he said, leaning against the banister, cool as ever.

"Then what do you want, Greg?" I asked.

"I wanted to stop by and check on you," he answered. "I know that things have gotten rough between you and Mitch lately," he said, his eyes locked on mine.

"Huh? *Lately?*" I responded sarcastically. "Is that what Mitch has been telling you?" Without waiting for him answer, "So what if they are, Greg? What if things are rough? How does that concern you?" I countered, my anxiety clearly showing.

"Jay ..." he implored.

"Don't call me that," I corrected him.

TEN

"I've been there for you before ... and I want to be there for you again," Greg whispered. "You deserve better than this," he said, taking a step up.

I backed away. "Greg, that was a long time ago. And though, yes, things aren't good between Mitch and me, and yes, I'm lonely, maybe lonelier than last time, I'm just not going to make the same choice this time around. I know this may sound absolutely crazy to you, but I'm really trying to lean on God to get me through this," I said, trying to sound more confident than I was feeling. But it was killing me. We had stolen one kiss and several long, comforting conversations, some fifteen years ago, just before Steven contacted me again. It was a mistake. We agreed not to tell Mitch, since the two of them were supposed best friends, but it hung in the air like a ghost whenever the three of us found ourselves in the same room together.

Just being in his presence, him saying these words that I wanted to hear, brought out a longing in me that made me feel weak, again, after all this time. In fact, I swore I could hear a voice taunt me, *Go ahead ... tell him you want him too. Shut up,* I fought with myself.

"Jay, I ..." Greg said, snapping me out of my headiness.

"You need to go. Please, before Mitch or the kids get home. Please, Greg. And please don't come to check on me again," I finished; now holding back tears.

He looked at me for a few moments then said, "Alright, Jules. I hear you. But if Mitch ever hurts you, if you ever need anything, please call me." He turned and walked back to his car without waiting for me to respond.

Please don't come back ... because if you do, I just might take you up on your offer, I thought, knowing how weak I really am these days. I am much too desperate for my own good.

ELEVEN

"Thanks for seeing me on my own, Dr. Grant," I said, taking a seat in the center of the loveseat.

"Absolutely, Jules. What would you like to discuss today?" he asked as he sat down across from me.

Confession: I like when Mitch drinks, I thought. *More to the point, I like that Mitch drinks. I don't like what it does to him, per se, but I have come to relish the gap that it has put between us. I don't know what I'd do without that gap. I can blame everything on that gap.*

"I'm trying to reconcile how to live my life when it's full of conflict," I said, shifting in my seat to block the sun from my eyes.

"Alright. So, you'd like to work on some conflict resolution techniques?" he asked for clarification.

Ha! No, I wish our marriage would crumble around us once and for all, and that conflict would work itself out to its honest end for a change, I mused with a barely visible smirk. "Not exactly," I responded with a small laugh. "What I mean is that I have many conflicts in my life, as in, I feel one thing but for reasons I sometimes can't pinpoint, I must live another thing."

"Example?" he asked while writing something in my chart.

"I try to honor Mitch's wishes, for instance, to not tell the kids some of his secrets about work, about the accident, about his drinking, but I'm dying to lead a life of authenticity. And it's difficult to honor

ELEVEN

someone that you resent from here to next Sunday," I finished with a coy smile.

"Ahh," he said, nodding. "Other examples you can think of?" he asked. *Do therapists do that to stall?*

"Well, I have to stay married when I don't want to. I try to be kind and hold my tongue when there's so much I want to say, so much I want to yell. I'm working on not acting out of anger and I really do hate conflict, but it seems that I am just so very angry, like all the time. I'm fiercely independent and yet feel really quite controlled by Mitch. I am working on my marriage, but I would give anything for my marriage to just disappear. In other words, I feel one set of emotions but must live out an entirely conflicting set of actions," I finished with a deep sigh. The sigh was not of weariness or of resignation. It was actually a sigh of relief for speaking my truth out loud to someone who I'm paying not to judge me.

"Who says you have to stay married?" he asked, leaning forward in his seat.

"My faith," I said, my mind flashing to Greg standing on my porch steps just yesterday. "I want out," I stopped myself. "Most of the time, I want out. But my faith, my church, the Bible I say I believe, my friends, my children, everybody, me. This is why, up til now, I've stayed married," I answered.

"Does Mitch know how you feel about all of this?"

"I feel like I've said it all, but even if I haven't, my crying myself to sleep most nights should be some kind of tip off to him."

"Your husband should care that his beautiful wife is sad," Dr. Grant said. I narrowed my eyes a bit. Did he just hit on me? No, I'm sure that's just what counselors do; it's their job to make their clients feel better.

"Well, I don't think I'm being unfair to Mitch when I say that I honestly don't think he cares about how I feel at all."

"I'm sorry to hear that," he said.

"After all these years, it's kind of funny, but I still believe in miracles. I believe completely that Jesus could heal this, I just don't know if he's going to. And seeing how much time has gone by, it's not looking like he will."

Dr. Grant said, "He?"

"Right," I said, "Jesus."

"Jesus doesn't have anything to do with this," Dr. Grant said. "And what I mean by that is this: The healing of your marriage does not depend on what Jesus will or won't do, as he is always ready and willing to help. The healing of your marriage completely depends on whether or not Mitch will cooperate. And, of course, you being able to let go of your bitterness, because a bitter heart is a set-in-stone heart, and that's where you seem to be living right now."

The sting took me by surprise. "I don't consider myself bitter."

Silence—that awkward, therapy kind of silence. "Okay, so I'm bitter. But if I am, I certainly have plenty of reasons to be. So, now what?"

"Well, we need to take a look at what you feel you can change about your situation so that you are not leading such a conflicting life, so that your bitterness is not driving your choices. What are some things you think you can change?" he asked, pen poised.

Therapists.

Therapy gets me all stirred up, makes me feel worse sometimes. Driving home, my mind was filled with a million obsessive thoughts.

It is clear that my cold, hard, closed-off-to-Mitch heart is considered disobedience on my part. Dr. Grant encouraged me to try to open it up to Mitch, even if I don't want to. Because, he said, it's the right thing to do, the obedient thing to do: the thing that will show that I did all I could and all I was told, the thing that will leave me clean before God if all goes south, the thing that will bring me peace. I do not want to open my heart to the man who has hurt me so deeply and repeatedly and who doesn't seem to care. But I do want God's full smile on my life. So, how do I do this?

I've got ten thousand days of lies to untangle, ten thousand days of truth to recover. I've been lied to, a lot. There are the standard lies. Like the innumerable *no's* to the question, "Are you drinking again?"

ELEVEN

And then there are the ones that took a bit more determination and forethought to pull off like, "I'm going to my AA meeting," only to find a receipt date-and time-stamped for the liquor store, coincidentally right at the same time as that meeting.

I think back to the advice I received of not getting worked up about all of Mitch's lies. *What?* How does one not get worked up about her husband lying to her, like most of the time? What I don't think anyone really understands is that when I am lied to about the drinking, it feels like everything else just might be a lie too. Is he really going to Greg's? Is he really going into work? Is that coffee in that mug? Or coffee and gin? Or just plain gin?

And then there are the other, more subtle lies that pervade my heart. He tells me he loves me. But does he really? When we are lying in bed and his hand is on my back and he tells me he's sorry after yelling at me earlier that afternoon, does he mean it? Is it the alcohol that called me *stupid* or the alcohol that is saying *it's sorry*? Does Mitch even know the truth anymore? I know I sure don't.

One of the ladies at church has this mantra: "Trust the man, and he will become worthy of your trust." And I have tried. I find a bottle or a receipt, and I confront him and he will lie or not lie and say he is sorry or not say he is sorry, and the bottles and receipts will go away and he'll treat me really nicely. He'll say sweet things or I'll get flowers. I might even get a greeting card, one that sounds nothing like our relationship or like what would come out of my husband's mouth, with *Love, Mitch* scrawled at the bottom. And a few days, or maybe even a couple weeks go by, and I'll acquiesce to sex. And the next day, it will be as if nothing wrong had ever gone down. He's done acting sorry and trying to make it up to me. I'll be left on my own to rebuild the trust.

I started picturing it like a wall of bricks. Every time there is a lie, or a discovery of contraband, the wall explodes sending bricks all over the place. But, then there are the apologies and honeymoon period, and I picture myself bending down, picking up a brick, putting it into place, tamping down the mortar, repeating "trust the man" mantra. But a few months later, there is another explosion.

But somewhere along the line, I have realized that the wrong person is rebuilding that damn trust wall. Mitch should be the one putting each brick back into place, securing it by telling the truth time and again, by being open to someone asking him the hard questions, being the opposite of defensive, filled with humility, knowing that it was the least he could do.

But he never has. Not really. I have never once seen follow-through with that man, never truly have seen a repentant heart. I never really saw humility that lasted for more than a few minutes, where his hand wasn't forced.

But you know what? I'm not going to build that wall anymore. It's not my job, and it never has been. But that said, *Today Jesus, I say that I will try to open my heart to Mitch. I will protect it from him hurting me continually, yes, but I will not let his hurtfulness further jade me or provoke me to anger or action; I will not stand in the way of the Holy Spirit's full working in my heart and life. I will do this for you alone. Show me how to do this. Show me what this means. Please take this as a sacrifice of worship. I cannot do this without you. Help me open my heart beginning now, even if the results aren't what I want, even if I get hurt even more. I love you. Amen.*

I stood at the kitchen window watching Mitch and Jordan playing basketball. I could hear their words between shots. Neither of them talk much to me so the only way I can find out what's going on in their heads is by eavesdropping. I'm not proud of this; I'm just stating a fact.

Jordan sank the perfect shot, no backboard, no rim. "Good job, Babe," I whispered.

Mitch, "You released the ball too late."

Shut up, Mitch. Encourage your son. Jordan smiled and laughed. He passed the ball to his dad and walked back in the house without a word to him.

"Hey, great shot."

ELEVEN

"Dad didn't think so. This is why I can't learn anything from him."

Caught off guard, "Do you mean like learn how to do stuff?"

"No, like as an example."

"Oh, Jordan …" I'm about to apologize for Mitch again. "You know you can tell him he hurt your feelings, to be easier on you."

"Mom, I just smile and laugh. When someone hurts me, I just smile and laugh. It's what I do. This is all just a charade. Besides, I don't even like him, so why should I care what he thinks about me?" He didn't wait for me to answer.

※

Mitch was gone for the afternoon, running errands, so I asked the kids to meet me in the living room. "Am I in trouble?" Jordan asked, flashing a grin.

"No, Dear, but you will be if you don't get in here," I smiled back.

Jesus, I need words. "I want to talk to you about something important. You have both talked to me about these things over the past year or two and I have never been prepared to offer you solid answers. I'm still pretty shaky about this subject, but I feel it's beyond time that you know a few things," I looked at them both in the eyes, trying to gauge if they were tracking with me. They seemed to be. I took a sip of my water and continued.

"Your father and I have a difficult relationship. I am so sorry for my part in that and for how it's hurt you over the years. I grew up like that and I never, ever wanted to do the same thing to my own children. But sometimes people repeat what they've seen, even when they hate what they've seen. Does that make sense?" I asked.

They both nodded, not saying anything.

"Okay, good. Now, there are some things that are passed on from parents to kids physically or genetically. Say, eye or hair color. There are some things that are passed on emotionally or mentally, like that both Dad and Jordan love sports, or Macey and I both like to keep a journal. Then there are some things that are passed on because of environment, basically what you're seeing as you're growing up, like being frugal or how to cook or how someone expresses joy or anger," I said. "Still with me?"

"Yeah," Macey said, looking at Jordan. He nodded, still quiet.

"Well, your dad 'has something,'" I said with air quotes, "that could be passed down to you genetically and environmentally, experts don't completely agree on the how, but that it is an alcohol abuse problem," I said, wincing. I paused, waiting for the kids to run out of the room or begin to sob.

"And?" Jordan said, as in, *so?*

"Well, there is no *and,* I just need you to know for a several reasons. First of all, he has mood swings, and they're usually tied to when he's had something to drink. Secondly, you need to know that you can tell him you don't want to get in the car with him if you think he's been drinking. And thirdly, you both need to be very careful around alcohol, because you may be prone to abuse. You also need to know that he doesn't drink because of either of you, or because of me. He still loves you very much, and it's okay to still love him and respect him. In fact, you can think of it as someone with diabetes or who has seizures, it's now out of his control, but it's important that we know about it. He has never meant to hurt any of us, but I believe he's beyond being able to stop on his own, and I also don't think he believes he has a problem. We don't agree on that part. Do you have any questions or anything you want to say?" I asked, imploring them with my eyes.

"This isn't exactly new information, Mom," Jordan said, looking almost annoyed that I took up so much of his time.

"I think what he means is that we kind of had an idea already, Mom, but we both appreciate you talking with us about it," Macey said, ever the big sister.

"There's something else. Though this really should be coming from your dad, I don't think he has any intention of telling you, and you're both old enough to know what's really going on with his job. He's been on leave since May. There was an accident, a plane went down. Two people were killed, and it was on your dad's shift." I kept barreling through, not looking either of them in the eyes. "He's being

ELEVEN

sued by the families of the men who were killed, and it's going to trial."

"Oh my gosh, Mom. That's awful. Dad must feel terrible. Is this why he's been drinking?" Macey was panicked.

Jordan, "Is Dad going to jail?"

"Why didn't he tell us this? Is he scared? Did he know the guys who died?"

"Okay, calm down. Yes, Dad feels horrible about the accident; it is an absolutely horrible thing that happened. I don't know why Daddy drinks, he's been drinking for a very long time, but stress usually makes drinkers drink more, so I'm sure this has added to it. We won't know about Dad's consequences until after the trial. I'm sure he didn't tell you because he's ashamed. I'm sure he's scared. And no, we didn't know the two men."

We sat in quiet for a few minutes.

"Listen, guys, I know this is all so huge, what I just dropped on you. This is way bigger than a regular teenager should have to handle. I'm going to ask you to not talk about this to friends, but if you need to talk, you can come to me or Lauren, or I've got a good counselor we can go to. I'm just so sorry. I'm so sorry this is your life right now. It's too much."

"We'll be okay, Mom," Macey said. She wiped tears away with the back of her hand. Who was she trying to convince, me or herself?

"Okay then," I said, letting out a breath that I felt like I'd been holding in since deciding to tell them days before. "Let me pray for you guys. God, I come to you and lift up my children to you. Thank you for creating them. Thank you for making them both so strong. Jesus, I ask that you will protect both Macey and Jordan from any kind of addiction, that you will make them both strong against temptation, and that you will bring healing, peace and some joy to our family. Please walk us through this super hard time. We don't know what's coming ahead for us, but we are choosing to trust you even when we can't understand. We love you. Amen."

"Amen," they both said. Jordan stood up, "We done?"

"Yeah, go ahead," I said, hitting him with a pillow.

"Love you, Mom," he said, bending down to give me an awkward hug.

"I love you, too, Jordan."

"Thanks, Mom," Macey said. "I know that was hard for you," she kissed me on the top of my head. "If there's anything I can do, please tell me, okay?"

"Of course, Honey, thank you."

You did the right thing, sweet girl.

Thank you, Jesus.

TWELVE

"The website said it would be down the stairs and to the left," I said to Lauren. "And hey, thank you so much for coming with me," I told her, as we walked into the church basement. "And thanks for driving so far, I wanted to make sure no one would recognize me under the circumstances with Mitch's case," I said.

"You bet," she said, giving my arm a squeeze. "Let's do this thing," she said with her typical go-get-'em grin.

I just shook my head and smiled. "Yeah, let's do this thing," I said quietly. I couldn't believe I was walking into an Al-Anon meeting. This was not my idea of a good time. But if it helped my mom, it might be able to help me. I was hoping for some ideas to try to get Mitch to stop drinking.

The room was set up with folding chairs in a big circle, about twenty or thirty people milling around, chit-chatting, laughing. *Why are they laughing? I thought these people are supposed to be all sad and depressed.*

Lauren and I took two seats by the door, glanced at each other and smiled. "We've gone a lot of weird places together," she leaned over and whispered, "but this one takes the cake." She got the laugh she was going for.

"I know," I said, "I totally owe you one," I winked.

TWELVE

A woman with a pink cardigan took a seat at the head of the circle, holding a notebook open. Too perky in my estimation, she welcomed us and said, "We who live, or have lived, with the problem of alcoholism understand as perhaps few others can. We, too, were lonely and frustrated but, in Al-Anon we discover that no situation is really hopeless, and that it is possible for us to find contentment, and even happiness, whether the alcoholic is still drinking or not."

What? Okay, this is crazy talk. If I come to this group, I'm going to learn to be content and happy, even if Mitch never stops drinking? Whatever, I thought, starting to shut out the woman's words.

She continued by sharing that finding solutions that work for us and bring us peace starts with our own outlook and tweaking our perceptions. "You'll be surprised how much a shift in attitude can do."

My attitude? MY attitude? What about HIS drinking? This is ridiculous. I shifted uncomfortably in my seat.

"Things can only get better. It's hard to live with an alcoholic, harder than most people understand outside these four walls. Our emotions take over our thinking, we try to control situations, and we become difficult to live with ourselves."

I beg your pardon but my thinking is crystal clear, and I am not DIFFICULT TO LIVE WITH! I laughed out loud once I realized what I just thought. Lauren shot me a look. I mouthed, "Sorry," and gave her a weak smile.

"Al-Anon takes its principles from AA, and we try each day to relate them to our lives. Going through the steps that alcoholics all over the world have gone through to reach sobriety is both humbling and mind-opening."

Wait, I have to go through the twelve steps? I'm so outta here, I scribbled on the back of a receipt and handed it to Lauren.

She wrote back, "You're not going anywhere," and gave me that just-keep-an-open-mind look of hers, so I relented.

I squirmed through the next hour, listening to one person after another talk about, not the alcoholics in their lives to my surprise and slight disappointment, but about how they were applying the steps to their own lives. It was simply bizarre. It wasn't anything like I'd thought it would be. For one thing, I was looking for someone to tell me how to get Mitch to stop drinking. That didn't happen. For another thing, it was occurring to me how much I've been reveling in the role of martyr, and I wasn't finding this to be the hotbed of victims I'd been hoping for. I kind of had the feeling that I wouldn't get a lot of sympathy from this group. But, if I stuck it out, I might get some hope. If I stuck it out.

My mind wandered to last night when Lauren and I saw a surprisingly morose movie. It left me with such sadness and this deep longing. I came home to find Mitch asleep on the couch, and so I went to bed alone. Again. Mitch had come to bed hours after I had fallen asleep, per usual. He was reeking with alcohol, again, not out of the ordinary. And it woke me up as it tends to do, not him coming to bed, but the actual smell. But this time, instead of an instantaneous nausea sweeping over me, my sadness and longing intermingled with my sleep, and half dreams left me with a comfort the moment I smelled that smell that I've come to hate. And I reached for Mitch, propelled by my acute longing for connection and comfort. When I realized that's what I was doing, I stopped myself and immediately began praying that the smell of alcohol never bring me comfort again, no matter what I'm feeling. I begged God to make sure it always repels me, no matter what that would mean for my relationship with Mitch.

The rest of the meeting ended up flying by and the same lady from the beginning flipped a page in the notebook and read, "In closing I would like to say that the opinions expressed here were strictly those of the person who gave them. Take what you liked and leave the rest. A few special words to those of you who haven't been with us long: Whatever your problems, there are those among us who have had them, too. If you try to keep an open mind, you will find help. You will come to realize that there is no situation too difficult to be bettered and no unhappiness too great to be lessened."[2]

I just sat there. Confused. Stunned. Moved. And something I never in a million years expected to feel: *at home*.

TWELVE

Lauren nudged me out of my daze. "Jules, this nice man wanted to know if we have any questions," she said, pulling me up by my arm. "So, do you?" she prodded.

"Oh, thank you. No, I think I'm good for now. Just sort of need it all to sink in a bit, but thank you," I answered. He handed me a few brochures, and then Lauren and I walked out.

When we got in the car, she asked, "So, what did you think? I can usually tell what you're thinking but I'm pretty stumped right now," she admitted.

"Ummm …" I said, then stopped. I took a deep breath and stared out the window.

"I know it was kinda corny, but I thought everyone seemed really genuine, and people laughed a lot more than I thought they would," she said. "Jules, what is in your head?" she repeated.

"I'm thinking I just might be one of them," I said with a nod toward the building. "And I think that I'll be going back," I finished with a small smile and a sigh.

I was in the bathroom putting towels away and heard, "Hey, got a minute?" I positioned myself behind the door. I could see Macey lean against the doorway to Jordan's room. They didn't know I was there. "So, what did you think about everything Mom said?"

"I don't know. I mean, I guess I'm not surprised, are you?" Jordan.

"No. I've been watching Daddy drink in the garage for a while now, but I guess it was easy to pretend it wasn't that big of a deal. Having Mom put it into words made it more real, if that makes sense."

"Yeah, I know."

"I'm just afraid that whenever I think of Dad, I'm going to think about his drinking. I just don't want that to stalk me the rest of my life, you know?"

"He's still Dad. Just a buzzed out version of him," Jordan laughed.

"That makes me feel a lot better. Glad we had this talk, little brother," Macey laughed and rolled her eyes.

There's a conversation I bet they never thought they'd have.

"Where've you been?" Mitch asked first thing as I walked into the kitchen after Lauren dropped me off.

"I left you a note," I said quietly. "I was at a meeting with Lauren," leaving out one fairly key detail.

"What meeting?" he said, with his hand resting on the note, completely oblivious. He walked over to the sink bumping his hip on the island and staggering a few inches.

I took in a deep breath. *Jules, this is not the time to tell him you were just at an Al-Anon meeting. He's already been drinking this morning. Who knows how he'd react?*

"A small group at church," I answered, not quite lying.

"Where did you put yesterday's newspaper?" he slurred, changing subjects.

"I'm pretty sure it's in the magazine rack in the living room," I said, "where I always put it," finishing, under my breath.

"What did you just say?" he snapped.

"Nothing," I said quickly, this time definitely lying, as I put the group brochure in my folder on the counter.

"Don't be such an ass," he said, and walked out of the room, careening into the door jam.

I'm an ass, now? I sighed. *Yep, that's about right*, I thought.

Last night I dreamt I was working an event where about five things were falling apart at the seams. My hands were full, literally and figuratively. I looked over and saw Mitch standing there, leaning against the bar, supposedly waiting for me.

I walked over and he said, "You've kept me waiting."

I replied, "I'm working. I didn't know you were even coming here. I didn't know you were here," I apologized. He walked away in a huff. I am a disappointment to my husband even in my own dreams. How do I even begin to undo that depth of pain?

Instinctively, I began rubbing my neck and said out loud to the air, "I hate this."

TWELVE

"You hate what?" Macey asked curiously.

I jumped. "Oh, Honey, you scared me," I said with a nervous laugh. "I didn't know you were standing there."

"What do you hate, Mom?" Macey asked me again in a soft voice, moving closer to me.

"Mace, oh nothing, just having one of those mornings," I lied. "I'm sorry that you heard me say that," I said.

"That's okay," she said as she started making a sandwich. "Want one?" she asked me.

"No, thanks. Hey, I just tried out a new small group thing this morning. I think it might help with some of our family stuff. Do you maybe want to go with me when I go back next week, just to check it out?" I asked.

"Sure," she said, "if you want me to."

"Well, I do want you to, and I think you'll get something out of it, but I don't want you to do it just for me, okay?" I asked.

"Okay. I'll go for me, then. I promise," Macey said, walking over and giving me a hug. "I love you, Mom," she whispered.

I was thinking about how much I've damaged Macey and Jordan because of the marriage they're growing up under, and I felt God say to me, "Every day you have stayed married is a day that you have loved your children more than yourself."

"I love you, too, Honey," I whispered back, a tear running down my cheek.

106

THIRTEEN

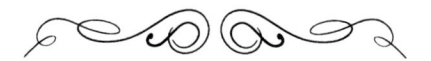

It was another night of struggling to fall asleep. I'm exhausted. Why can't I just fall asleep? I can't remember the last time that I closed my eyes at night and didn't think about being the wife of a man who drinks. I used to think about writing assignments, or the funny things my kids said, or daydream about an upcoming vacation. But now, bam, eyes close, obsession begins. I'd pray. Pray he'd hit me, just once … or cheat … anything to give me an official, "biblical" out. I'd wonder how much the kids knew. Will he make it home in one piece this time? Will he embarrass me at another event? Is he hiding anything else? Will I ever know the truth, the complete truth? Will we ever have a solid relationship? Will this ever not be the most consuming thing in my life?

And then one night it hit me, mid-obsession. Being a man who abuses alcohol isn't even the most important thing about Mitch's own life, so it totally shouldn't be the most important thing about my life. But how do I change that?

Do you ever feel like you're living someone else's life? As in, there's no way that the life you're living is actually your own? Like, how in the world did the benign choices you made all those years ago lead to you crying yourself to sleep every night?

> Will you replace the lost years that the enemy, my sin, his sin, our words have stolen? Redeem them, at least. And

THIRTEEN

strengthen me, Lord, for the next forty or so years. Passion, intimacy, partnership, romance, even honesty might not be in my future, but you are. You are my future. And because of that, I can do anything. Oh Jesus, please be my husband.

~~~

The next morning, I woke up with a bit of a bounce in my step. Hope had snuck in and buoyed me up sometime during the night, quite unexpectedly.

"Good morning, my sweet boy," I said with a smile when Jordan walked into the kitchen. "Want me to make you something for breakfast?" I asked him.

"I'm good, Mom, thanks," he said suspiciously. "Why the good mood?" he asked.

"Can't I actually wake up on the right side of the bed once in a while?" I asked with a laugh.

"Sure, Mom," he said, "But I'm running late, and I won't be home til late, too, because I've got my first detention tonight," he said, looking down.

"It's okay, Hon. We all make mistakes, trust me," I said. "I'll have some dinner for you when you get home," I said. "I love you, Jordan," I added.

"Love you, too, Mom," he said, grabbing a banana and his backpack, and heading out the side door.

Mitch walked in and stopped Jordan. "Hey, want to shoot hoops after school today?" he asked.

"Can't today, Dad, but thanks. Maybe this weekend, okay?" Jordan answered, catching my eye, and headed out just as the bus pulled up.

"I made you some coffee," I said to Mitch, as I picked up my folder and a huge pile of papers I hadn't gone through in ages. I knocked a cup of pens off the counter, and while bending over to clean them up the folder fell out of my hands, spreading all its contents on the floor between Mitch and me. He bent down to start helping me clean up, and there on top of the pile was the Al-Anon brochure. I hurried to pick it up and shoved it back in the pile with as much guilt as an alcoholic watching a secret bottle of gin fall out of a grocery bag. *Did he just see that?*

He stood up quickly, walked to the coffee pot and poured a cup, not looking at me. "Thanks for the coffee," he said sharply, and walked out of the kitchen.

Great, that's just what I need today, I thought. *Strike one, and it's only seven o'clock,* beating myself up. *Jules, what did you hear just yesterday at that meeting? You can't change him, and don't let his mood ruin your day,* I encouraged myself. *Trying …*

I jumped on my bike with a resolve to have a good day. Could it really be that easy? Just tell myself to have a good day and then, voila? I guess we'd see.

I pulled up to my father's house with butterflies in my stomach. I hated that I knew this thing about him now, something I'm sure he would not want to revisit. For goodness sakes', it just occurred to me that I didn't even know if he still drank! I shook my head, trying to dislodge the parade of thoughts as I walked up to the door. I knocked and waited for him to answer.

"Why didn't you just come in," he asked sternly, making me feel like a ten-year-old all over again.

I walked inside, not knowing how to answer. "Sorry," I said, feeling off kilter. I removed my jacket and plopped down at the kitchen table. "Thanks for the tea," I said softly, seeing that Dad had already prepared it. "Sorry I was a few minutes late," I added.

"How's it going?" he asked gruffly, sitting across from me, holding onto his thick coffee mug. Staring at the mug I thought, *is coffee really all that's in there?* "Earth to Jules," my father said, snapping his fingers.

"Sorry," I said for the third time in under two minutes. "Just a little spacey today, I guess, got a lot on my mind," pronouncing the understatement of the year.

"What's up?" he asked, fidgeting with the small sugar packets in the bowl in the center of the table. He was arranging them by color.

THIRTEEN

He only liked real sugar, but he kept the pink ones around in case. That was actually very thoughtful of him.

"I've been reading Mom's letters pretty slowly," I said. He nodded. "I got to my tenth birthday letter," I said, looking to see if he'd know what I was referring to.

"What did she say in that one?" he asked, stirring his coffee absentmindedly.

"You wrote that one," I reminded him.

He looked up, startled. "Oh, I pretty much forgot all about that," he said. His look turned to something between curiosity and mild concern. "So, what did *I* say then?" he asked.

"You don't remember at all?" I replied.

"I think I tried to be clever about double digits, but beyond that, it's kind of fuzzy," he answered.

I couldn't tell if he were sincerely forgetful, or purposely trying to dodge the subject. *Jesus, do I keep pressing on this?* I prayed quickly and silently. I felt a nudge to keep going and took a deep breath.

Looking him in the eyes, I said, "You said we were having a hard time as a family, that you were sorry for all the arguing, and that you thought I was growing up to be a lovely girl."

I looked down when I said those last words, oddly embarrassed. Perhaps hoping for some reaffirmation from this sixty-something man to this forty-something daughter.

"Oh," he replied, still stirring, still looking down. "Well, I was sorry. I felt badly about how you were coping with things," he said, re-crossing his legs. "Did you read any farther than that?" he asked, seemingly more for his sake than mine.

"Yeah, I've read a few more," I said and stopped. *Do I tell him that Mom said he drank? That Mom finally found help? Jesus …*

Not now, not yet. It's okay. I felt God say.

"They're all pretty much about how I was doing in school and with friends, stuff like that," I continued, sparing his feelings, sparing mine.

"Hmmm, well, your mother did have a knack for details and loved bragging on you," he said with a wistful smile, now looking out the window as if he were watching her in the backyard.

Shifting gears, "Any news on Mitch's case?" he asked abruptly. He didn't like the focus on himself, and apparently didn't like all this talk about Mom either.

"We haven't heard anything in a little while, actually," I said. "It's almost too quiet, you know?" I continued.

"Well, let me know," he said quickly.

"I will, Dad. Listen, I need to run. I've got a big event coming up and need to spend some time on it today," I said, standing and putting my jacket back on.

"What organization is it for?" Dad asked, surprising me with his interest.

I walked over to the sink and rinsed out my tea cup, saying over my shoulder, "My favorite. They're doing amazing work in the area of child trafficking," I said. "I'd love to see, firsthand, what they're doing someday …" my voice trailing off.

As I reached the door, "Jules, I'm proud of you," he said, looking down, brushing imaginary crumbs off the table.

I stopped and teared up. I quickly wiped the tear before turning back to him, "Thank you, Dad. That means a lot to me," I said. I walked out, got on my bike. It was turning out to be a good day after all.

When I got home, I decided to sneak in another couple letters before hitting the office, sort of my reward for having the guts to talk to my father. I got all comfy on the living room couch after starting a fire.

My fifteenth birthday was more about me and Steven than anything else. My mom couldn't get over that I already had a boyfriend. Her protectiveness shown through. But something in my sixteenth letter took my breath away.

> Do you remember the time your father accidentally drove into the garage door? Do you remember what we told you?

THIRTEEN

> I told you that Daddy was tired and that it was snowing hard and the car slipped on the icy driveway, but that wasn't what happened. I lied, Julianne, to protect your father and to protect you. Because the truth is your father drove home drunk and drove the car straight into the garage without remembering to get out and put the door up. Al-Anon has been helping, but I really don't know if I should do this anymore. I don't know if I can.

I remember that night. I thought it was hysterical, except for the part about not having a car for a few weeks to practice my driving. And it turns out that Mom was thinking about leaving him, even after getting help. Apparently, it wasn't helping enough.

I don't think people get how hard this is. I mean, reading this letter, I actually have compassion for my father. He must have been hurting, or something, to drink like this. But for those of us who live on the other side of it, who live in the hard and the hurt, and choose not to numb ourselves in order to get through it. Well, it's a whole different kind of pain. And sometimes the numbing just happens on its own.

"Dammit!" I heard Mitch yell from the other room, being startled out of my daydreaming. Then I heard a banging, the sound of a phone being repeatedly jolted onto the receiver.

I quickly got up and walked into the kitchen. "What's wrong?" I asked, almost afraid of the answer. Mitch was pacing, breathing quickly.

"Mitch, what's going on?" I repeated, standing in the doorway.

"That was my lawyer," he hissed. "The two families are suing me jointly," he said, "and the trial starts on Monday," he finished.

He looked exhausted and frightened.

"I'm so sorry, Mitch," I said, walking towards him. Part of me wanted to hold him, and part of me was holding on to too much hurt to be of any comfort to him, so I stopped myself. "Is there anything I can do for you?" I asked, not fully meaning it, I'm sorry to admit.

"You can get your story straight about the night of the accident," he said, as he brushed past me.

I leaned against the counter, repeating his words in my head. The straight story was this: He had been drinking before he went to work that night, and I knew it. *What am I supposed to do with that, Jesus?*

⁂

I stood in line at the grocery store, unloading my cart onto the conveyer belt, my mind completely occupied with Mitch's case and my perception of what happened the day of the accident. I happened to catch a glimpse of the woman in front of me putting one of the separator bars between my items and hers, and then I noticed her do it again, separating one other item. Two receipts. I've seen that before, no big deal. From my quick first glimpse, the lone item was a bottle of mouthwash. It wasn't until I finished unloading and settled in behind my cart, waiting for my turn, that I realized it was a bottle of vodka. I looked at the woman checking out. She was making small talk about her husband being away a lot in the evenings these days because of being a tax man and how she gets so bored so she bakes, bakes, bakes. *And drinks, drinks, drinks apparently,* I thought to myself. She was talking fast and loud, definitely nervous.

I stood frozen, my eyes shooting back and forth between the bottle that now separated my groceries from hers and the woman with small beads of sweat forming on her forehead as the cashier called for a price check on Skol. A wave of nausea swept over me as I wondered how many people had stood behind my husband, watching him get two receipts. "Put it back," I whispered. I hadn't meant to say it out loud, but it turns out I did. She looked at me, not sure if I were talking to her. "Put it back," I said more clearly this time.

"What?" she asked.

"The vodka. Do you actually think your husband will not know that you drink just because you get two receipts? Put it back. Don't do this," my voice escalating out of my control. The woman looked around nervously, smiled at the cashier and nodded toward me like I was losing my mind. "He knows what you're doing!" I actually yelled at

THIRTEEN

her as she quickly pushed her cart toward the store exit. "I've probably met your husband in Al-Anon!" The cashier eyed me, shook her head a bit judgmentally, and asked for my grocery card. I walked right on past her, leaving all my items on the belt unpurchased, crying the whole way to my car.

Macey was sitting cross-legged on the ledge of the fireplace when I got home, with college catalogs spread out all around her. She picked one up, flipped through it, put it back down. She rearranged them in what appeared like a random order.

I was walking through the living room when I heard her mutter something under her breath and toss one into the fire. "Whatcha doing, Honey?" I asked, kneeling down beside her and picking up one of the catalogs.

"I'm sort of trying to decide which college to go to," she said.

"*Sort of?*" I asked. "I take it as a *no* if a catalog finds itself in the fireplace?" I laughed.

"I'm not sure that I should go to college," she blurted.

"Mace, what are you talking about?" I asked.

She sighed. "Mom, things seem bad here. I don't think I should leave now."

"Oh, Honey." I didn't say anything for a minute, closing my eyes.

"Are you mad?" she asked.

"No, I'm thinking about what to say," I smiled.

"You don't have to say anything," she said, fingering one of the catalogs.

"Okay, here's what I want to say. Things, as you put it, are not great around here. But you sticking around, when life is waiting for you, won't change that fact. I love you. I love that you want to stay. But Honey, these problems are mine and your father's. You need to do what God is calling you to do, which I'm pretty sure does not include a lifetime stint as an Old Navy cashier," I said, reaching over to tuck some stray hair behind her ears. "Not that I haven't come to rely on that family discount," I added.

"Crud! I tossed my first choice into the fire!" she laughed. "Oh well. Hey, can I tell you something I've been thinking about?"

"Absolutely."

"I think I want to study something about international relations or something related to relief work, but I haven't wanted to let myself go there in my heart because I haven't been sure for months about whether or not I should even go," she said, looking down.

"Honey, first of all, please don't hold things like that inside for months at a time. I'm here and I'm a really good listener. I remember what it was like trying to choose colleges and majors and stuff like that, so use me, okay? And I think you would be amazing at that kind of work. You have such a huge heart. The mom in me wants to tell you to look for relief work here in the suburbs," I said with a smile, "But more than what I want, I want God's best for you. I really do. So pray about it, make your pros and cons lists, and then just go for it," I said. "Alright?"

"Alright," Macey said, stacking up her catalogs and putting the fire out.

FOURTEEN

Mitch's lawyer, Mr. Stockton, prepped me on the phone before the trial. He gave me an idea of what questions might be asked and told me that it would be a bench trial, meaning no jury, which he thought would come as a relief to me. "Don't be nervous," he said. "You'll be great."

I muttered, "Easy for you to say," as I hung up the phone.

"Mrs. Millhouse, we're starting with your husband's testimony, then yours. The families have requested that Mr. Millhouse not be present in the courtroom at any time except when he's on the stand," Mitch's lawyer explained to me the morning of the trial.

We were in a small room, just off to the side of the courtroom, and Mitch was uncomfortably pacing behind me, making me more anxious, if that's even possible.

"Remember to answer only what is being asked of you and no more," Mr. Stockton said, leafing through some papers in his briefcase. "Do you have any questions?" he asked us without looking up.

Mitch shook his head *no*. "No," I said, my voice shaking.

He looked up at me. "Are you alright?" Mr. Stockton asked.

"Not really," I answered. "But would you expect any different?" I asked, fidgeting with my purse strap.

FOURTEEN

Mitch was leaning against the wall, his arms crossed. His stare gave me chills, and I had to look away. I had been praying about what to do, what to say. If I backed out, which I'm not sure I even legally could, it would look horrible for Mitch's case. If I lied, I'd be in contempt of court and do even more damage if caught. But if I'm outright asked if I thought Mitch had something to drink that night before he went in to work, and I told the truth, what would that mean for Mitch? Could my words actually make things worse for him?

I've heard that we always have options, that we're never trapped by our circumstances. But right now I was looking down the barrel of three really bad outcomes. A rock and a hard place seemed like kids' play right about now.

"I'll get you some water, Mrs. Millhouse," Mr. Stockton said, picking up his briefcase. "You both wait in here for me to get you when it's time," he said, walking out and closing the door behind him.

Mitch sat down at the table across from me. I didn't like the look in his eyes. "I know this is a strange time to bring this up, Jules," he said, leaning forward, "But I know that you know that I drink sometimes."

Sometimes? I shrieked in my head. "Okay," I said slowly, not sure where he was going with this.

"I have a feeling that you think I had something to drink the night of the crash," he said, playing with his wedding ring, "And I think you should consider that you don't really know that for sure before you go on the stand. There's really no way for you to know that," he said. "Would you agree?" he asked, looking at me now.

I hated when he did that. When he'd paint this logical-sounding picture and back me into a corner with a yes or no question. "Well, the report said …" I started.

"That's not what I'm asking you. I'm asking if you agree that there is no clear way for you, Jules, to know for certain if I had something to drink before I went to work that night. Yes or no?" he asked, ever the persuader. He should've been a lawyer.

"Technically, I guess that's true," I said, that familiar feeling of doubting my intuition bubbling up inside me. I knew what the report said, that there was some alcohol in his system and that traces of an antidepressant showed up, as well. And I remember thinking back on the day of the accident, before he went into work that he might have seemed a little off. But other than the smell, the slight slurring, the glassy eyes and the temper, I did not have proof.

I say *other than* like I didn't just rattle off a laundry list of some pretty telling symptoms, but really, in our house, it's an invisible affliction. Unless I saw him drink directly out of a bottle of something, I don't really know for sure if he's had a drink in the past fifteen years. *Technically.*

My shoulders slumped. Well, I guess that's my truth then. If asked, *when* asked, I will say what I know. Nothing less. But nothing more either.

Mr. Stockton opened the door and poked his head in. "Mitch, let's go. You're up." I followed them in, Mitch walking to the stand, Mr. Stockton taking his place behind the defendant's table. I sat in the galley.

"All rise. The Honorable Judge Alan King presiding."

Mitch was sworn in, and after answering the foundational questions, the prosecuting attorney sprung to life.

Jesus, please help Mitch tell the truth. Please. Make him do the right thing. For all of us.

"Mr. Millhouse, were you working on the day of May 26?"

"Yes."

"What time did your shift begin that day?"

"Three p.m."

"So, what time did you leave your house?"

"About 2:15 p.m."

"And had you had anything to drink before you left for work?"

"Coffee and orange juice," Mitch answered with a smirk.

Mitch, what are you thinking? This isn't a game!

"Mr. Millhouse, let me rephrase the question as I must not have been clear enough. Did you have any alcohol to drink that day before you left for work?"

"No."

FOURTEEN

"Interesting. And were you on any medication that day?"

"No."

"Really? Then can you explain why the toxicology report found traces of Sertraline, an antianxiety medication, along with alcohol in your system?"

"No."

"No? Are you saying the toxicology report was inaccurate?"

"Yes."

"Mr. Millhouse, this toxicology report was run twice, and the results were agreed upon by three doctors."

Mitch, "I don't know what to tell you."

How can you possibly think talking to him like this is going to win you any points?

With a smile, "I've got nothing further, Your Honor." He shook his head and sat down.

Judge King, "Mr. Stockton?"

"Nothing for Mr. Millhouse, Your Honor. If we could take a brief recess, I'm ready to then bring Mrs. Millhouse to the stand."

"Granted. Fifteen minute recess."

Mr. Stockton turned to me, "Mrs. Millhouse, you're up next. Mitch, you'll need to wait in the hall. This shouldn't take too long."

I looked at Mitch and gave him a half smile as he walked out. What had he just set me up for? I felt nauseous and wanted to be anywhere but there. *Jesus, this is it. Please help me do this. Please give me the right words and your strength.*

I felt a hand on my shoulder and turned to see Lauren sitting behind me. "What was that all about?" she asked. "It's like he doesn't get how serious this is."

"I know. He's just digging himself deeper."

Mitch's lawyer gave me a look. I rolled my eyes at Lauren and turned around, feeling chastised. Knowing Lauren was there, I felt a little bit better already and when the judge called us back to order, I walked through the small swinging door that the bailiff was holding open for me.

"Place your right hand on the Bible. Do you swear to tell the truth, the whole truth, and nothing but the truth, so help you God?" he asked me.

With my hand firmly on God's word, "I do."

I walked to the witness stand and sat down. Behind the prosecuting attorney were two wives—make that two *widows*—and their teenaged children. I gasped quietly. I hadn't seen them before, when I first walked in. My heart broke for them all over again. My husband, in his sin, in his sickness, whatever you want to call it, did this to these families. He may not have meant to, but his choices led to this nonetheless.

"Good afternoon, Mrs. Millhouse," the prosecuting attorney said as he stood up and buttoned his suit coat. "Please state your full name for the record," he said.

"Julianne Camille Millhouse," I said, my voice faltering.

"What is your relationship to Mitch Millhouse?" he asked.

"I am his wife," I answered quietly.

"I'll need you to speak up just a bit, please, Ma'am," he said.

"Sorry," I said, a bit louder, leaning closer to the microphone. "I'm his wife," I repeated.

"What does your husband do for a living?" he asked.

"He is an air traffic controller," I answered. *So far, so good*, I thought.

"How long has he been doing this?" he asked.

"About twenty-four years," I answered.

"Mrs. Millhouse, I'm going to ask you some questions about the night of the accident. On May 26, were you at home?" he asked.

"Yes," I answered.

"And did you see your husband leave for work?" he asked.

"No," I said.

"Why not?" he asked.

"I was in my office at home at the time that he left for the day," I said.

"Is that typical?" he asked.

"It depends on his shift, the time he needs to leave, and what I've got going on that day," I answered, in too much detail.

FOURTEEN

"Did you see your husband at all during the day before he left for work?" he asked.

"Yes," I said.

"How long before he left did you see him?" he asked.

"I would say maybe an hour prior. We had lunch together as a family," I answered again too lengthily.

He smiled. I think he liked me. I kept giving him more information than he was asking for. I tried to focus on the exact wording of the next question.

"And what would you say his disposition was at that time, Mrs. Millhouse?" he asked. *Oh boy*, I thought. *Here it comes.*

"Objection, Your Honor. Mr. Millhouse's *disposition* is not relevant," Mr. Stockton said as he stood up.

"Granted," the judge said.

"Let me be more specific, Mrs. Millhouse," the prosecuting attorney said. "Did you see your husband have an alcoholic beverage anytime that day before he went to work?" he asked.

"No," I answered honestly. *Please don't ask me what I thought, though*, I thought.

"Alright," he said slowly, his eyes narrowing. "In your opinion, do you think he had been drinking before he went to work that night?"

Before I could answer, Mr. Stockton interjected, "Objection, Your Honor. He is leading the witness."

"Overruled. I'll allow it," the judge said, looking at me. "Go ahead and answer, Mrs. Millhouse," he said.

I took a deep breath and locked eyes with Lauren. She gave me a small smile and a nod. *Jesus*, I prayed, *what am I about to do to Mitch?* "There is no way for me to know for sure, but I had been suspicious that he had been drinking that day," I answered honestly, letting the breath out.

People began to whisper. "Order," the judge said, banging his gavel.

I looked at Lauren and she smiled at me again, only bigger this time. I'd done the right thing. Okay, then why was I so scared? I kept scanning the crowd for Mitch even though I knew he was told not to come into the courtroom. *If he had just heard what I said, he'd ... well, I don't know what he'd do.*

"I have nothing further, Your Honor," the prosecuting attorney said confidently, sitting down.

"Defense, would you like to cross examine?" the judge asked Mr. Stockton.

"Yes, Your Honor," he said, as he stood up.

"Mrs. Millhouse, you said that you had been suspicious that your husband had been drinking the day of the accident, correct?" he asked, repeating me word for word.

"Yes," I said.

"And yet you didn't try to stop him from going to his job as an air traffic controller, knowing lives would be at risk?" he asked pointedly.

"I …" I started, then stopped. I didn't know what to say. *Did he just accuse me of not stopping this plane accident? Just think.* "Well," I started again, "I had learned long ago that my interfering never worked anyway."

"What do you mean?" he asked.

"In other instances when I had thought he'd been drinking and I tried to stop him from driving, it didn't go well," I answered.

"In what respect?" Mr. Stockton pushed.

"He'd get angry," I replied. "So, eventually, I just stopped."

"Um-hmm," he said. "Mrs. Millhouse," he continued, looking at a paper in his hand and not at me, "Would you consider yourself an honest person?" he asked.

"Excuse me?" I asked, confused.

"Do you usually tell the truth?" he asked.

"Yes, I'd like to think so," I answered, not understanding where he was going with this.

"Do you hide things from your husband?" he asked me, now looking directly at me.

"I don't think I know what you're talking about," I replied, feeling my face become warm.

"Is it true that you began an affair with an old boyfriend, and hid this from your husband?" he asked.

FOURTEEN

Now the prosecuting attorney stood up, objecting, "Your Honor, he is badgering this witness, *his* witness, I might add, and I don't see how this pertains to the case in the least," he said, still standing.

"I suggest you get to your point quickly or you come up with a new line of questioning, Mr. Stockton," the judge said, leaving me out to dry.

"What I'm getting at, Your Honor, is that Mrs. Millhouse may not be the most reliable witness or the best source to judge someone else's personal practices, especially a man she clearly doesn't love enough to be faithful to," he said.

"Can I say something?" I asked, my voice quivering. I felt betrayed and blindsided. Mitch had sold me out. I couldn't believe he shared something like that just in case I didn't back him up.

I didn't wait for permission before proceeding. "I did not have an affair. I contemplated starting one, but, first of all, that was over fifteen years ago, and, secondly, I told my husband about it and came clean. I have nothing to hide," I said, attempting to clear my name.

"I have nothing further, Your Honor," Mr. Stockton said smugly, getting the judge to doubt my credibility just enough to satisfy himself.

"You may step down, Mrs. Millhouse," the judge said. "I've heard the testimony, and I will be entering my decision on Monday at 9 am."

Without another word, I was ushered out of the courtroom by the bailiff. Lauren joined me in the hallway. "I'm so sorry, honey," she said as she hugged me. "Where's Mitch right now?" she asked.

"In there," I said, pointing to the room where he was waiting. I was vacillating between seething with an anger that bordered on hatred and a level of embarrassment that left me wanting to run and hide. "You know what? I'll literally just cause a scene if I talk to him right now. Would you take me home?" I asked her.

"Of course. Let's get outta here," she said, with her arm around my shoulders. "It'll be okay," she said, trying to reassure me. But I just wasn't buying it. This felt beyond the scope of okay.

Lauren and I drove around for a while, and after she dropped me off, I took a long shower and put my pajamas on. I still had a couple hours before the kids would be coming home from school, but I had no idea when Mitch would walk through that door. Though, at this point, *never* would be too soon.

I curled up on the couch with my Bible and did one of those pray-and-open-it-hoping-it-lands-on-something-good things that I like to do when I don't know what to look up, hoping for something even remotely relevant to my situation. Psalm 109 (NIV) didn't let me down. I gasped as the words jumped off the page, as if reading my mind.

> When he is tried, let him be found guilty …
> May his days be few;
> may another take his place of leadership.
> May his children be fatherless
> and his wife a widow …
> May this be the LORD's payment to my accusers,
> to those who speak evil of me.

Lord, I'm so sorry for wishing for these things. I know that's no better than what Mitch just did to me, but I almost can't help it. I want him out of my life, in whatever form that may take. I'm so sorry.

> But you, O Sovereign LORD, deal well with me for your
> name's sake;
> out of the goodness of your love, deliver me.
> For I am poor and needy,
> and my heart is wounded within me …
> With my mouth I will greatly extol the LORD;
> in the great throng I will praise him.
> For he stands at the right hand of the needy,
> to save his life from those who condemn them.

> Jesus, I feel condemned. I made a mistake, but I confessed
> and stopped myself, and it was years and years ago. He has

FOURTEEN

>never let me live that down, even with all the hiding he's done to me. Just like your Word says, I am needy, Lord. My heart is wounded, broken into a million pieces. I'm not sure I can forgive this. Please save me from the one who condemns me with his lies, his words, his actions. My condemner is my husband. I need your help. My enemy is my husband.

Just as I closed my Bible and finished praying, I heard the kitchen door open. Mitch was home. I stayed on the couch, my back to the kitchen. I closed my eyes and breathed in deeply, slowly. Horrible words were being screamed in my head, and it took everything in me not to run at him and start pounding on his chest with my fists. Apparently that time with Jesus didn't temper my anger. I didn't say a word, didn't make a move. Just waited to see what Mitch would do or say, if anything.

He walked into the living room, tossing his keys on the sofa table behind me. The icy clattering of the keys hitting the wood startled me. He came around to face me. "I cannot believe you said you thought I'd been drinking on the day of my accident! Are you kidding me? Do you really think I would drink and then go to work? You were all I had. You were the only person left who believed in me! If I'm found guilty, it will be 100 percent on your head! I can't even look at you right now," he yelled, and turned to walk away. "I'm packing a bag and going to stay with Greg for a while. And don't worry about our next counseling appointment. I'm going to take care of that one on my own," he said as if he were punishing me.

My eyes got bigger. *He* was leaving *me*? *He* was accusing *me* of betraying *him*? *He* was mad at *me*? *He set me up!* I felt my heart race and I stood up.

"Don't you dare walk out of this room!" I yelled back. "Mitch, you told your lawyer about Steven and told him to use it against me if my testimony didn't go the way you wanted it to. In other words, if I told the *truth*! You humiliated me up there! I was only trying to do the right thing." I felt myself get a little dizzy from not stopping to take a breath so I half sat, half fell back onto the couch, and stayed there.

I steadied myself for a moment, and looked up at Mitch who was staring at me with such rage.

"And as far as not believing in you or whatever, there is evidence that you were intoxicated. You *were* impaired on the job. You made a mistake that killed those two men. I can't magically just believe in you. You have lied about this. You have lied about so much else! I don't care if you stay or go, but you don't dare make this about me screwing you over, because, Baby, you did that all by yourself," I yelled.

I stood back up and walked past him, sprinting up the stairs and heading to my bathroom for another Jesus fix. I shut the door behind me, and slid down the door. Once I hit the floor, the sobs came. Again. I must have fallen asleep from emotional exhaustion, because I woke up to find myself on my bathroom floor, the arm of my robe soaked from my tears. I picked myself up off the floor and went to lie on my bed.

I heard a faint knock on the door and Lauren stuck her head in. "Macey told me you were up here. Can I come in?" she asked, already in.

"Sure," I said, not bothering to sit up.

"Why are you lying here in the middle of the day, in your robe? And are you listening to your CD of sad songs again?" she asked me. "Why do you do this to yourself?" she questioned, coming to sit down next to me on the bed.

"I can't quite explain how it works but when I make myself feel as sad as I possibly can, I somehow feel better," I answered.

"Wow, Honey, you need help," she said, with a small smile.

"No kidding," I said, and closed my eyes. "What am I going to do? He set me up, Lauren. He told me that he blames me if he's found guilty."

"I don't know, Honey," she said. "I'm so sorry."

After she left, I headed downstairs. The kids were in the kitchen both working on their homework and Mitch was on the computer in his office as if we hadn't even had that conversation. *Why are you still here?* I thought. I sighed and asked silently for strength just to get through the evening, to stay married for just this one evening.

FIFTEEN

I EXPECTED THIS TO BE THE longest weekend of my life. This morning, though I anticipated the silent treatment at best, I received a hug and some casual conversation. Outwardly, to keep the peace, I went along. Inwardly I was screaming, *Words! I need words!* Like, *I'm sorry for being a jackass* or *I'm sorry for treating you like crap yesterday* or *can we talk about what happened*? Nope, just a swat on the tush: what every woman longs for.

I told Lauren the other day that I'm not sure if I prefer Mitch sober or drunk. However, I was rethinking that, and I've decided that I don't really prefer him at all, which is so very sad. Every night as I put myself to bed, my mind wanders down the road, and I can't help but wonder how in the world the next year or so of my life will turn out. Will we be together celebrating a victory, celebrating a miraculous and divine intervention, celebrating the year things turned around?

Or will I be, alone, celebrating the smaller, harder-fought win of making it through another year, on my own, despite my circumstances, in a tiny bit less pain, hopefully, with a tad more peace, whether or not the drinking continues, whether or not he this or that? Will I be grieving my reality with fewer tears, walking with my head held even just a little higher, finding purposeful outlets for my heartache, turning to more appropriate venues for my loneliness? Will that be what I have to look forward to this coming year? Or something else entirely that only God can see?

FIFTEEN

What is my fate for the next 365 days? Because, truth be told, the last, oh I don't know, eight thousand or so days, have been very, very difficult, very, very lonely, and very, very sad. And I'm just hanging on by a thread, an extremely thin, fragile, invisible thread.

※ ※ ※

Being in the courtroom the other day reminded me of our wedding. I had one of those fork-in-the-road moments just before Mitch and I exchanged vows. I was in the women's restroom of the courthouse, reapplying my lipstick for the fourth time in about five minutes, a nervous habit of mine I'd had since high school. This wasn't how it was supposed to be. My mom was supposed to be fluffing my veil, my father walking me down the aisle. I was looking at myself in the mirror. Now, there's looking at yourself while you apply lipstick, and then there's looking at yourself as if you're seeing this whole other person who happens to be you.

"Are you sure about this? You can still back out, you know. There's still time," I said out loud to my reflected self.

"It'll be fine," my reflection answered, almost too quickly, in a tone thick with persuasion. Then my reflection gave a nervous smile.

I took a deep breath and heard, as if there were a man standing behind me, "Don't do this." The voice was either God or my subconscious, but I swept it away with a fifth application of lipstick.

I looked myself in the eye and said, "Don't be ridiculous," then picked up my small bouquet and walked out.

I go back to that moment over and over. The entire course of my life could have been altered, could have been better, had I cut and run. But I'm not a runner.

※ ※ ※

The rest of the weekend was a blur of Mitch coming and going, me trying to bury myself in work. (He had apparently decided not to leave me after all, though he never actually told me this.) Of me trying to pretend he hadn't just sent me down the river. I watched Mitch slowly fade throughout the afternoon on his way to his preferred state of numbness. Slowly fade throughout our marriage is more like it, but I'm trying to just focus on the now. He went three days, best as I can tell, without a drop. But this afternoon, he is most definitely *off*. Unfortunately, his off has become his norm.

He is throwing me for a loop, though. He actually asked if I wanted to go for a walk. I agreed, though with inward resistance, and he held my hand. At one point, I actually jerked my hand away pretending there was a bee, then I shoved it in my pocket. Then that evening he brought dinner home from my favorite takeout place. So-called normal days totally unnerve me, especially in the middle of this craziness, probably because they are coming fewer and farther between lately. It's like I don't have a place in my head to put the normal days, the normal activities. They make me doubt the rest of my life, as if perhaps I'm just making some mountains out of a few tiny beer cans and a gin-and-tonic or two.

If I were a bit healthier or had some distance, I would know that this is what's called the honeymoon phase in an abusive relationship. But I'm not healthy or far enough away to know this yet.

I did know better than to enter into a conversation of any substance though, since he'd been drinking today, plus I didn't really have anything in particular to say to him, so I headed to my office to work on my next event for a little while. The kids were both away at friends' houses for the evening and I had some extra time and quiet on my hands, so I thought.

After hearing pots and pans clanking around, and even something crashing to the kitchen floor, Mitch came into my office and stood in the doorway, visibly agitated. I stopped typing and looked up.

"What's up?" I asked, trying to sound all casual and mask the utter irritation in my voice.

"What's up is that my gin is missing," he alleged.

"What gin?" I asked. I could not believe he just asked me that. It was a point blank admission. "I haven't touched it, Mitch," I answered with a sigh, my shoulders slumping. *Did Jordan take that too?* I couldn't even go there right now. My hand instinctively went to my neck and

FIFTEEN

started rubbing, a headache immediately beginning. I hoped that would be it and he'd walk back out. *Don't engage, don't engage*, I told myself silently. I stared at the computer screen but he wasn't leaving.

"Really?" he asked, "Because it was just there a few days ago, right where I left it...." His voice trailed off as he realized that he had just told his wife that he kept a secret gin stash in their kitchen. *Well played, sir,* I smirked.

Upset with himself and hoping to shift the laser beam of truth's light shining down off of himself and onto someone else, he chose to pick a fight on a totally different topic. "So, making any more life and death decisions based off of your mom's letters?" he said with sarcasm. He shifted his weight from one foot to the other, hoping the pointed change of subject would bring the control back to his court by upsetting me.

"I'm not making any decisions from my mom's letters, and it would mean a lot to me if you wouldn't talk about her or the letters like that," I replied, my voice rising, right along with my blood pressure. I'd been baited.

"Seems to me like you're making quite a few. You started going to that stupid support group of yours ever since you found out your mom went to one," he said. He had done it again, said more than he should have. I hadn't shared any of the letters' content with Mitch. He had to have found them and read them on his own.

"How do you know what my mom's letters say?" I yelled. Without waiting for his answer, "How dare you go through my things?"

"Have something to hide, Jules? *Again?*" he yelled back.

"No, Mitch, for the last time, *you* are the hiding one in this family!" I screamed.

My anger rose to match his. I could tell that I was about to lose it all over him. I knew I could stop myself, should stop myself. But here's the thing, I didn't want to.

Who did he think he was, accusing me of taking his gin, reading my mother's letters without my permission, talking to me with such contempt, when he was the one who was ruining our lives with all his lying and hiding and drinking? I wanted to scream out into the world that I was hurt and lonely and angry and sad, that I felt broken beyond repair. I wanted to scream out to other hurting women to hang in there because heaven will surely be better than this, right? *Right? It has to be!* I wanted to scream at Mitch that he has hurt me so desperately, and continues to do so in his lack of pursuing, in his lack of a spine, in his lack of taking this life and his marriage seriously. I wanted to scream out to him that he's missing out on so much more with me. Why can't he just see me, and love me, and stop hurting me? Why can't he just stop drinking, just stop hurting himself, just stop killing our family?

But, I knew I would never say any of those things to him. Not because I couldn't. Not because it would be inappropriate or harsh. No, because there would be no point. So, I screamed other things. Needed things. Hurtful things. *If Jesus were taking sides, he'd so be on mine on this one*, I thought to myself and smirked, knowing I wasn't being theologically correct. It helped me catch a breath. I think he mistook my smile for calming down.

I went in for the kill. "I threw out the roses you gave me last week," I said through clenched teeth. "I don't want your flowers, Mitch. And I don't want chocolates. And what was with that stupid bracelet?" I asked, not actually wanting an answer. "I don't want flowers; I want repentance. I don't want candy; I want you to stop lying to me. I don't want jewelry; I want to be able to trust you! I want a husband who isn't always drunk!" I was trembling. I finished with, "You may think you're trying, but when you keep doing all the wrong things, you might as well not bother with that other stuff at all!" Getting those things off my chest felt simultaneously delicious and horrifyingly guilt-inducing. "By the way, did someone tell you to do all this? I can't imagine you came up with it on your own." Without letting him answer, "Either way, just stop it, Mitch. *Stop.*"

He picked up the paperweight on my desk, the one my father had given me when he retired from the newspaper. He held it in his hands, moving it back and forth from one hand to the other. I couldn't tell what he was thinking. Honestly, I couldn't tell if he were thinking anything at all.

But then his back stiffened and his eyes zeroed in, and as if in slow motion, I watched him as he threw it against the wall. I froze as I heard a whirring sound while it missed my head by about an inch.

If he'd been sober, it would've hit me, I thought. *If he'd been sober, he wouldn't have thrown it*, I corrected myself.

"What the hell was that?" I whispered to him, to no one.

In the moments right after my husband acts unbecomingly, I die just a little bit more. I can go from working on a project, to a huge argument, to utter fear within seconds. I can go from, *This relationship is livable and I'm going to make it through another day being married* to *I want my marriage to disappear. I. Can't. Stand. This. Man.* Like, that (snap).

My heart was pounding so loudly I could hear it in my ears. For a few moments I just sat. I looked at Mitch. I looked at him with absolute hatred. I wanted him out of my life with everything in me. "Get out," I whispered through clenched teeth. *You make me sick.*

But then, something in his eyes made me soften my gaze, and I looked at him again, really looked at him. As angry as I was, compassion began to well up when I realized that he looked … scared. Of himself maybe.

He turned around and walked out without saying a word. Without, therefore, an apology. Without, therefore, making sure I was okay. I heard the door slam, then a few moments later, his car start and peel out of the driveway.

"And by the way," I said to the remnants of our worst argument yet, "Happy anniversary, Honey."

I sat shaking for a few minutes, waiting for my breathing to return to normal. Some branches of the weeping willow tree just outside my window swayed against the house. I wished the tree would just fall down around me. I let my head land on my desk, and all I could think was, *Jesus … help … Jesus …*

I dreamt that Mitch, Macey, Jordan, and I were taking a trip. We were on an airplane that was taking off from a ship in the middle of the ocean. As we were about to take off, Mitch pulled the clutch that stopped the conveyer belt that was supposed to lead us out of the belly of the ship, so instead of heading upwards to take off, we dipped into the water. Water crashed into the plane, engulfing Macey and Jordan, and then us. I could actually feel myself being underwater, but then the water receded, first off of us then off of the kids, who I could see swimming under the water. And though Macey immediately said they were both okay, I was horribly shaken and immediately realized, in the dream *and* then again when I replayed it in my head just after waking up, that the overwhelming chaos that we had just endured was all Mitch's fault.

When I woke up, the light had shifted, making it dark in my office even though it was just late afternoon by now. I must've fallen asleep for an hour or so, the argument adrenaline had plummeted causing an immediate exhaustion. I left the paperweight, broken in two, on the floor, along with the chipped paint and small pieces of drywall that had been knocked off.

I went to my bedroom, grabbed my mother's letters, and took off for the park on my bike. When I got there, I leaned my bike against a tree. I walked toward my favorite spot and laid my things on the bench. I looked around to make sure I was alone, and then I screamed as loudly as I could. I screamed as if I were being attacked. I screamed as if I were scared out of my mind. I screamed until my throat felt like fire. A couple birds flew out of the tree just overhead.

An immediate flood of guilt washed over me, as it does whenever I express my true level of anger. I go back and forth from knowing that I should know better, that I should work on just pushing it down, I guess, and keeping my mouth shut. But then I remember something Dr. Grant said, when I confessed in embarrassment all of my pent-up

FIFTEEN

anger. "Twenty years of deceit is hard to just get over." Yeah, I guess it is.

I sat down on the bench that overlooks the stream. I pulled out the last letter. I took a few deep breaths. I didn't want this to be the last one. But, I so hoped that what my mom would say would be just what I needed to hear today, in the middle of this mess I had found myself in again, or more to the point, still.

> Dear Julianne,
>
> You are seventeen years old today. I can't believe I get to be your mother! You are such a delight to me.
>
> You and Steven are getting ready to go away for college. I really like him, Honey. You two are a good fit, and he treats you so well. I know you've been together for a few years now, but don't rush in. You're still so young. Just make sure he's the one. Marriage is for a long time.
>
> Sweet girl, I've decided not to leave your father, after all. We're getting help and things are turning around a bit. I may never have the marriage that I want, and frankly, neither might your father, but we are going to keep trying. And I believe that God will honor this decision, at least I hope so.
>
> Life can be hard and messy, and all at the same time God is so good, even when you don't feel it or see it. Keep reaching for His hand. He is right there, my darling girl.
>
> Hugs and kisses and lots of peace,
>
> Momma

I stood back up, walking to the edge of the stream. My mind zoned out, not soaking in her words just yet. My eyes followed the path of one leaf heading downstream. When it got caught on a mossy rock, I noticed that it had started to rain lightly and that I was shivering from the cold, so I got back on my bike to head home. The chilly breeze cleared my head of the fog and, with crystal clarity, I began realizing a few things.

She had decided to stay. She had the choice to walk away. Part of her wanted to walk away but she put Dad first. She put us first. She put God first, ahead of what she wanted. *That was right for her, but I don't know if I can do that,* I thought to myself. *I don't know what putting God first looks like for me. It might look completely different for me.*

Your Word says to love with actions and in truth, not just with words. I think to love in truth might be to not just love someone based on their merit or your feelings. But on the truth that they are created in the image of God, that you call us to love, that we already have everything we need for life and godliness within us, that true love is Jesus laying his life down for us, that if we claim to love God we must also love our brother. But it could also mean to stand up against evil for the sake of the person committing the evil. Ugh, I just don't know.

Help me stay married for the rest of the day, just for today, Jesus.

"That's all I've got in me right now. And when I get to heaven, if you tell me, 'You know, you could've left him,' I'll be so ticked," I said out loud, trying to lighten my own mood. It didn't work.

I gathered my things and got back on my bike to head home. Tears began rolling down my cheeks as I pedaled. *God, I want to put you first, but …*

SIXTEEN

"Hi, I'm Jules," I said quietly.

"Hi, Jules," the group replied.

"I'm grateful to be here today. I've only been here a few weeks. When I first came here, I, well ... I didn't want to be here. I didn't think I needed it. I just wanted answers on how to make my husband stop drinking," I said.

People all around the group nodded in understanding, with some scattered, knowing laughter.

"But I am realizing that I need to take responsibility for myself. Just because I didn't cause my husband to start drinking doesn't mean I didn't make things worse by how I responded to him. My husband has not found sobriety. He doesn't even think he has a drinking problem, but I realize that doesn't matter as much as it matters that I change how I look at things. I've learned so much from all of you already, so, thank you."

"Thanks, Jules," the group said warmly. "Keep coming back."

The next morning, I was in the kitchen when Mitch walked through the door. He sheepishly said, "I've got some good news, and I've got some bad news. Which do you want to hear first?"

SIXTEEN

I didn't want to hear either. I was tired of this game, because it usually meant both were bad news. "Whichever you want to tell me first."

"The good news is we now have a really good reason to get that hairline crack in the windshield fixed."

"What happened, Mitch?" I asked with little patience.

"Well, it was really foggy last night, and I hit a lawn mower, and it sorta broke the windshield."

I walked to the window and saw a windshield that was being held together against the forces of gravity and reason, smashed into thousands of pieces. "Where did this happen? How? That mower must've come flying at the windshield to do that. Did you stop and talk to the owners?"

Silence.

"Mitch, it wasn't foggy last night. Let me guess, you were drinking and you ran into it, and, again, just guessing, you drove home without taking care of the damages. Am I close?"

"I'll need to use your car today," he replied without answering me.

"No. The kids and I are going to church, and I'm not going to drive around in your car. You made this mess; you need to live with the consequences."

I hate sitting here alone. Both kids are sitting with their friends, and Mitch hasn't joined us on a Sunday morning in months. This place used to feel like home, but the higher I put up my walls, the less of a sanctuary this sanctuary feels.

"I'll be waiting in the car," I text Macey and Jordan at the end of the service. If I can just get through the lobby without making eye contact with anyone. *Oh no. Please don't walk over to me. Please walk the other way.*

Crap.

"Jules, how are you? It feels like forever since I've seen you," Mara sweetly implicated.

"I'm here every week," I responded too sharply. I backpedaled a bit, "How are you?" hoping she wouldn't notice I didn't answer her question. I do this a lot.

"I'm fine. But what I really want to know is how you and Mitch are doing these days? I'm assuming better since you haven't asked for advice in a while …"

I made the mistake a couple years ago of sharing my marriage struggles with Mara. She's a few years older than me, and she loves God. I say it was a mistake because not everyone who loves God understands things like alcohol abuse. Not her fault, totally mine. I was naïve in who I looked to for help back then. She actually read through a book of the Bible and took notes on it, *for me*, then sent me the notes and how I could apply them all to my life. I was so hurt and stunned by her gall, I didn't speak to her for a year.

"Ummm, things are about the same," I lied, "but we don't need to go down that path right now." I begged her with my eyes to stop talking to me, to walk away. *You're suffocating me. You make me feel like a horrible wife even though I'm trying more than you'll ever see, or know, or give me credit for. You make me feel even more trapped than I already feel. I already know what you're going to say, and I already know that you think it's all my fault. Please, stop talking.*

"Well, I think about you two all the time. I just know that if you were to show him more grace everything would turn around. You just need to make your home a place he wants to come home to, a refuge. You need to praise him more."

I looked at her blankly. Had I just asked her for advice? I don't think I did.

"And you know what they say, 'Be an angel in the kitchen and a devil in the bedroom,'" she finished with a giggle and a wink. She walked away before I could slap her. I mean, before I could *thank* her.

I just stood there with my mouth hanging open, my eyes narrowed, and my hands tightened into fists. I had no words. Well, I had no words I could say to her in church. Things like, *who do you think you are?* And, *what the hell?* I swear it was one sentence away from Mitch

SIXTEEN

getting a pat on the back and a knowing look that said, *No wonder you drink, you're married to her.*

But wait, though. Why was I continually being blamed for Mitch's sin? Why was no one at this place calling him out on it? Why was I the one with the list of things to change, while he kept getting the grace card tossed at him? Really? I just needed to thank him for mowing the lawn, make him a pot roast and put on something sexy, and then things would be all rosy? Listen people, tried and failed, okay?

And everybody wonders why most of us answer *fine* when asked how we are by fellow churchgoers.

~~~

It was too cold to be sitting outside, but the sun felt magical on my face. I'm a spring girl and would sit on this porch all day long if I could. I rocked, staring out, looking at nothing. The only way I could get that church conversation out of my head was to reminisce. My mind was scooting from one thought to another.

Why did I walk away from Steven? Why did I leave a man who truly loved me? Yes, almost twenty years later, I still think about this, still consider this my greatest regret.

Why didn't I walk away from Mitch before it was too late? Why did I stay with a man who didn't love me? Why did I stay with someone who sucked me dry? Why did I marry a man who already hurt me?

I think there's a place in every little girl that needs to be drawn out. She needs to be called out into her true beauty and freedom. And if that doesn't happen, like it didn't for so many women I know, we walk around carrying this empty cup, clanging it against steel bars.

We drop our own dollar bills into our open guitar cases to attract attention, hoping to convince and fool the passers-by that we're something to behold, that we're worth the time to stop, and listen, and reward. But when the people keep on walking, we lower the price. We'll take just about anything. Nickels and dimes will suffice. Anything. We'll beg and borrow and steal. We'll be grateful for crumbs.

Please, fill up my cup. Please, see me. Please, say I'm beautiful. I really do have something precious to offer you.

I don't recall being studied and found lovely. I never once felt adored. The part of me that was supposed to be brought to life never saw the light of day. And then, it was too late. And once I became accustomed to loose change and candy wrappers, I not only started giving myself away for free, in bits and pieces, but I allowed myself to be emptied out, to be misused. I still do.

I walked away from a man who truly loved me because I had no idea how to accept his love. I walked away from a man who truly loved me because I had no idea how to love him back. I looked into his eyes one night and could not physically hold his stare. The intimacy of that one moment fell outside the borders of what my heart could comprehend. I had no response other than to break the stare, make a joke, press in for a kiss that wasn't reciprocated.

And then I moved on to—and stayed too long with—a man who didn't love me, who treated me as if I were a burden, an annoyance, because that was all I knew. I only felt comfortable with the shallow. I only knew the ting of the cup filled with spare change. And I keep rattling it, waiting for it to be filled. Every day. Still.

I'm exhausted. All I want to do is sleep. That can't be normal. I should probably ask Dr. Grant about that.

Is Jordan going down Mitch's path? Is there nothing I can do to stop him? Will his every feeling stay submerged until it's too late when it will come out sideways, cutting himself on its way out with destructive choices?

Will Macey ever be able to find a good man? Will she suffer from giving her heart away too soon like me, or standards so high and fragile that no one will ever measure up?

We are in trouble, Jesus. How many more years are you going to require me to beg you for your help?

"Jules?"

I tensed up. I didn't know Mitch was home let alone standing there.

"Can I sit down?"

I scooted over without saying anything or looking at him. I thought he was going to talk about court, logistics about when we should leave

SIXTEEN

to find out the verdict tomorrow. He cleared his throat, something he does only when he's about to say something he doesn't want to say.

"I'll do whatever it takes to win you back."

What? These words were fifteen years too late. I needed to hear this ages ago. It's too late now. I turned to look at him, looking right through him. I felt nothing for him, and then I felt guilt for feeling nothing for him, especially as I had just recently told Jesus I would open my heart to my husband even if it killed me. But I had moved beyond anger and hate, to indifference and nothing, just nothing. Why was he saying this now? Was it his fear? Was it another honeymoon stage? Was it guilt? He was sitting uncomfortably close. His breathing was labored as if he had just been running.

He said it again, "I'll do whatever it takes."

I smelled alcohol on his breath with each syllable he huffed out. It was the alcohol talking, not a sincere husband filled with remorse and humility.

"Mitch, do you not know by now that I don't listen to a word you say when you're intoxicated?" He got up and left me there, rocking, holding my empty cup.

※

I went to my father's to see if he needed anything from the store. Okay, actually to see if maybe he'd say something nice to me again, as I'm especially empty and raw today. Those few words he said to me as I was leaving last time were sustenance to me. I'm totally scared about hearing the verdict tomorrow, so yes; I'm basically running to my daddy, okay? Will this hyper-awareness of my deficiencies ever fully go away? Or will I always feel just left of center for the rest of my life?

"Mitch stopped by this morning," he started. "He dropped off those hedge clippers he borrowed last fall. By the way, what the hell happened to his car?"

"What did he say happened?"

"He told me a rock hit it when he was following behind a semi."

"Well, there you go." I didn't like lying to my father but I didn't see the point of getting into anything with him about Mitch either.

"That's a load of crap. What is going on between you two?"

"Dad, I don't really want to get into it. Can we talk about something else? Please?" I leaned against the counter, closed my eyes and rubbed my temples.

"Okay. What do you think the verdict is going to be?" He sat down at the kitchen table.

"Can we talk about a different something else?" I sighed.

"I don't know why you put up with it. I thought you were stronger than this. Your mother wouldn't have put up with anything like what I've seen you take. But, I guess she did have more backbone than you."

"Wait, *what?* Are you telling me that I should leave Mitch and if I were more like Mom, I would've left a long time ago?"

"I'm just saying that you sure seem to let him walk all over you, that he seems to be about to take you and the kids down with him and you're letting him, and that you haven't seemed happy in ages."

I drew in a deep breath. I looked at the clock and watched the second hand click thirty times before saying anything.

Speaking in a whisper, "Dad, you don't know the first thing about my marriage. I know what it's taken to stay married for thousands of days when I haven't wanted to. And I know what it's taken to stay put because I was trying to give my children stability. And I know what it's taken to attempt to keep my vows when pretty much every day I find myself praying for an out. What I am living each day is not cowardice. I am not a wimp who is afraid to leave. I have stayed on purpose, not out of a lack of a backbone. And by the way, from what I can tell, Mom *did* put up with a lot."

With my hand on the door, "And to think, I actually came here this morning thinking I could get something from you, some kindness, especially with what's going on. Instead, you just made it perfectly clear that you do not approve of my choices or accept me for who I am. Good to know, Dad." Slam.

Dammit, anybody else want to tell me that I'm doing everything wrong? Step right up.

SEVENTEEN

*T*HE JUDGE POUNDED HIS GAVEL to restore order and he cleared his voice. "I have heard all of the testimony and considered the evidence. Mr. Millhouse, do you wish to address the court?"

Mitch stood up, buttoning his suit coat. I have never seen him this visibly afraid in my life. "No, Your Honor." He sat down quickly, his chair screeching across the floor.

The judge resumed, "In the case of Thompson vs. Millhouse, I find the defendant, Mitchell Randall Millhouse, guilty of manslaughter." Macey gasped and began to cry. Jordan put his arm around her. I stiffened my shoulders and sat a little taller. Mitch slumped. "In the case of Foxworth vs. Millhouse, I find the defendant, Mitchell Randall Millhouse, guilty of manslaughter. Sentencing for both carry a minimum term of seven years in prison. A sentencing date will be scheduled for early next week. Mr. Millhouse, you are not to leave the state during this time," the judge said with a final bang of his gavel. He stood up and walked out.

Mitch stood up and turned to look at us without saying a word. He looked at me. He reached for my hand but when I didn't take it, Macey reached out and took it instead.

SEVENTEEN

We drove home in silence, except for Macey's sniffling and her attempts to hold back her crying. Jordan continued being the strong, quiet one, his arm staying firmly fixed around his sister's shoulders.

Mitch stared out the window, not saying a word. Though I was driving, my mind was not there in the car with my family. It was up ahead a bit, envisioning the preparations of sending Mitch off to prison for an as-of-yet undetermined amount of time. *What is Mitch thinking right now? Will my kids make it through this? Will they be scarred for life by their father's mistakes? Will I be raising our kids alone for the rest of their childhoods? Would we write each other? Would I visit him? We didn't talk now, would we talk then? Would we be able to move past this? Would Mitch recover from being branded guilty of manslaughter? What would happen to him in prison? Who will he become? Would his addiction heal itself or go underground, only to come out a raving lunatic at the end of the whole thing? And when he came back home, then what? Life as usual?*

We pulled into the driveway. We all got out of the car, the kids going to their rooms, Mitch and I standing in the kitchen.

"Can we talk for a minute?" he said, sitting down at the table.

"I guess." I was too tired for one of our talks, but it was the least I could do for the guy, considering the circumstances.

"I talked to our financial adviser last week. Our mortgage should be paid off in six years. I've set up automatic payments. And the kids' college funds are taken care of, well, most of it at least. They may need to get part time jobs for some of the extras, but, I think they're set."

"Thanks." I didn't know what to say. I didn't know he'd been working on all that.

"You don't have to wait for me, you know," he said with a small smile, the first I'd seen in a long time. He was baiting me, looking for reassurance. It was something I didn't think I could give him. I didn't want to lie but he had already been beaten down so much today.

"Oh, don't worry, I won't," I said with a laugh, in a way that he'd hopefully take as teasing. But you know what they say, "There's a little bit of truth in everything we say," and frankly, in that moment, I didn't know if I would be waiting around or not.

I jumped on my bike and headed to the park again. I had to get out of that house. It felt quieter and colder than usual. Mitch was following me around, his neediness landing on me like an itchy wool sweater that I couldn't rip off fast enough. I know I sound heartless. Sometimes, I think I am.

Parking my bike, I headed to the stream with my Bible and journal. Only just barely situated, "Jules?"

I looked up and saw Brandon and Celia. They're the new elder couple at church, and I've been meaning to give them a call and beg them for help ... I mean, thank them for taking on that role. We used to be in a couples group together years ago, but we haven't had a deep conversation in a while.

"Hi guys, how are you?"

"Pretty good. Enjoying the day, huh?" Brandon.

"I wouldn't quite say that. I'm not sure how much you've heard about our situation ..." I paused, hoping they'd fill in the blanks themselves.

"About Mitch and the case? Yeah, we heard. We're so sorry," said Celia. I could tell her heart was breaking for me just thinking about it all.

"Well, Mitch received his verdict today. Guilty of manslaughter on two counts. I know I'm selfish but I just had to get out of the house. It was all closing in on me there."

They sat down on the bench next to me, one on each side. Brandon put his arm around my shoulder and Celia reached for my hand. I didn't want to be this girl, the needy one, the one who doesn't have her act together after years of getting so good at pretending that she did. But that's the girl I am now. All it took was those small gestures, the light touches of connection, and I was crying uncontrollably. They sat there, quietly, waiting for me to say something.

They started to pray, one after another, "Lord, please be a comfort to Jules right now. Please protect Macey and Jordan. Please help Mitch

SEVENTEEN

have the strength to get through this, to endure what this might do to his reputation …"

At this, it occurred to me that they probably thought my sadness was related solely to Mitch's sentencing and that they assumed he was actually innocent.

"About Mitch …" I stopped myself. I had been burned before: first with Mara, then with Pastor Aaron. I had shared my heart, asked for help, and was patted on the head and sent back into battle with a list of things to do to be a better wife. I didn't know if I could open up again. I was too tired, too scared, too embarrassed, too ashamed. I didn't want a problem like this. I didn't want to have to say these words to anyone else ever again. I was done.

Tell them. I sent them here. Really? *Really.*

Deep breath. I closed my eyes.

"About Mitch. I'm not just upset about the sentencing, though that's part of it. What you don't know, what almost no one knows, is what is really going on with us." With that, I told them everything. I told them about the drinking, and the lies, and the windshield. I told them that he had been drinking on the day of the accident and that he was found guilty because he *was* guilty. I told them about the fighting, and my yelling, and the paperweight being thrown at my head. About me finding Al-Anon and trying to figure out what my part is and how much I really am to blame. Even about asking for help from church and not really getting it.

And then I stopped talking. And when I stopped, I was emptied out. I had no more words. I had no more energy. I just sat there on the bench with Celia looking out over the water while Brandon put my bike in their trunk. They walked me to their car and drove me home, though I actually don't remember much after all my words stopped pouring out.

Except for this, I remember them walking me up to the house and Brandon looking me in the eye and saying, "We do not blame you for Mitch's choices. We will walk you through this. We will help you. You are not alone, Jules. We hear you. We get it. Things are going to change."

I walked into my home, numb, exhausted, at peace, and with some hope. I wanted to head straight to bed, but remembered a load of laundry I had left in the wash. I moved slowly through the house, not wanting anyone to know I was home, cowardly mouse that I had become. As I made it to the bottom of the basement stairs, my breath stopped.

One light bulb hung exposed from the ceiling, its chain dangling from the breeze coming in from the vent. Mitch was alone. He sat on the floor leaning up against the wall in the corner. His shirt was wrinkled. His tie was undone. He looked homeless. Hopeless. There was a bottle of gin in his hand, along with one lying by his feet. He held a marker in one hand while a single tear slid down his cheek. Without him seeing or hearing me, I backed up the stairs and went to bed.

EIGHTEEN

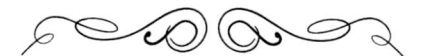

The next morning I woke up knowing that every single thing in my life was different. My husband was headed to prison. Macey was walking wounded. Jordan had found one more reason to hunker down inside himself.

And I was, well, I was everything. Every emotion I had ever had was felt, all at the same time. I had never experienced this level of fatigue before in my life. I was oddly hopeful at Brandon's assurance of help and intervention, though terrified at what that would look like, how much more work and honesty were up ahead for me. And I was ever-so-slightly disgustingly looking forward to Mitch being gone, though I couldn't say those words to a soul.

My legs were heavy, and I wasn't sure I could even make it down the stairs, but as I plodded into the kitchen, Macey walked in just behind me, holding a cup of coffee. Her eyes told me all I needed to know, that she hadn't slept at all last night.

I leaned in and held her, and she began crying into my shoulder. "It's going to be okay, Baby, it really is. We'll figure all this out." I whispered these things over and over again, not believing a word I was saying. How in the world would this be okay? Her father was going to jail for killing two men because he was drunk. This was insane, unfair, too much for a teenager to carry, that's for sure.

EIGHTEEN

"Have you seen Dad?" she asked me. "I didn't hear him leave this morning, but his car is gone."

"No, I just woke up. Last time I saw him was last night. I'm sure he just needed to get some space. This has got to be such a weight on him," I said. I actually felt sympathy for him. Truly, I couldn't imagine being in his position, guilty or not. The shame and fear must be overwhelming.

"Father God, we lift up Daddy to you right now. Please comfort him wherever he is, please remind him that you love him and we love him." Macey prayed. It's like her heart wasn't created to hold bitterness. He had pretty much ruined her life, at least changed it drastically in horrible ways, and all she could muster up was empathy and concern. She didn't get that from me, I'm afraid.

Mitch and I had an appointment with Dr. Grant scheduled for this afternoon, long before his trial date had been set. I didn't cancel it because I thought he might need it even more right now, that maybe he would open up. When he didn't show up back home or respond to my text reminding him of our appointment, I went on my own. I reasoned that I could use all the help I could get right now.

"Mitch not joining us today?" Dr. Grant asked as he looked over my shoulder into the waiting room.

"No. He was found guilty of manslaughter yesterday," I said before even sitting down. *Geez, Jules, way to ease yourself in.*

"Jules, I'm so sorry. How is he?"

"Ummm … I don't really know. I found him last night in the basement with a bottle of gin in his hand. He didn't know I saw him. It was the saddest thing I've ever seen. And then he's been gone all day and didn't even check in to say he wasn't coming with me here."

"Wow. Alright, then, let's talk about how you're doing with this. This is huge. It's like evil has entered your home."

"It's like *evil has entered my home*? Gosh, when you put it that way …" I laughed wearily.

"I'm sorry. What I mean is that this is above average on the horrible scale. You have an enemy, Jules, and he seems to have targeted your family with one hard thing after another. Or your marriage, at least."

"Is it weird that I find that reassuring? I mean, I'm not glad that I have an enemy or I feel attacked, but just hearing you say that my life is harder than the average hard right now ... well, it sort of helps me not feel so bad for feeling this darkness, this exhaustion. I seriously don't know how to get through this. I don't know how to get through each of these days. It's too hard. It's all just too hard. And my kids, I'm not strong enough to take care of myself right now, how am I going to get them through this?" I wiped tears away with the back of my shirt sleeve, frantically looking in my purse for tissue. Dr. Grant leaned over and handed me a few.

"Well, let's start at the beginning. Tell me, do you think the verdict was fair?"

"If you're asking me if I do, in fact, think he was drinking the morning of the crash, and if he is responsible for those two men being dead, *yes*. I'm not sure I'd have the guts to say that if Mitch were sitting next to me right now, but yes. He'd been drinking. His choices led him to do this awful thing to those men and their families."

"How do you feel about Mitch going to prison?"

"I feel horrible for him. I can't imagine what he must be thinking or feeling right now," I just shook my head in wonder, trying to find the words, picturing him again on that floor. I wonder how he's going to make it a day, let alone possibly years without alcohol. He practically needs it. *He does need it.* I don't say this out loud, though.

"You didn't answer my question. You just answered how you think Mitch feels. How do *you* feel about him going away?"

"Which answer do you want, Dr. Grant? The one that is expected of me as a good Christian girl, or the truth, the one that will make me look like a pathetic human being with no compassion and no heart?"

Dr. Grant looked at me without answering.

"I can't wait for him to be gone, okay? I was disappointed that the bailiff didn't take him right then and there. I wanted to pack his suitcase for him as soon as we got home, but then realized that he

EIGHTEEN

probably can't take anything with him." I looked at the pattern in the rug, tracing the lines with my eyes. I didn't want to keep talking but I also couldn't stop.

"I will not miss him. I cannot wait for the arguing to stop and to not feel compelled to look for receipts or bottles. I cannot wait for quiet. I can't wait to not be scared all the time, to not be sad all the time. I want him to be gone now. Is that what you want to hear? You going to write that down in my chart and share it with your colleagues at lunch? Tell them about the bitch who is actually happy her husband is going to jail?" I realized I was yelling. I didn't mean to be yelling. Dr. Grant started to write something and then stopped.

"I'm sorry. I'm so sorry. I have no excuse for yelling at you, or being disrespectful. Please forgive me."

"Forgiven. You're carrying a heavy load today," he said.

"I stepped on a rock when I was little girl. Well, more of a pebble, I guess. It cut through the skin and healed up all weird. Like, I can't see the scar anymore but can feel it on the bottom of my foot, where it went in. But here's the thing, I told everyone that the rock went in my foot and stayed there. And I told the story that way over and over, so many times, to the extent that thirty-plus years later and I honestly have no idea if there's a rock inside my foot or not." I let my shoulders fall.

I continued, "We were at a wedding once, this was about ten years ago, and it had an open bar. No big deal except that Mitch had just told me that he wasn't drinking earlier that week. And I happened to look across the dance floor and see him stand by a plant, drink something in one long gulp, throw the rest in the planter, and walk out the door. He came back a few moments later, in through the other entrance as if he'd just been to the restroom or something. When I brought it up later that night, he told me that if he didn't know better, he'd say I was bipolar by the way I was behaving. And I just added that to the list of lies that I took on as truth. According to him, what I saw wasn't reality, and according to him, I was basically crazy. He hadn't been standing by the plant, I hadn't seen him drink anything, and he had certainly not thrown anything into a planter. According to Mitch.

Just like with my foot, I think I've been telling my story in the same way for so long—that Mitch has been telling *my* story in the same way for so long—that I don't know what's truth anymore. Is there a rock in my foot? Am I crazy? No idea on both accounts."

"What do you think is truth?"

"I don't know. I've always wished Mitch and I could have a third party living in our house with us, listening in on every argument, on every conversation, someone who would look at both of us and say, 'Wait, that's not right,' or 'Jules, you're way off on this one, Mitch is telling the truth this time.' When it's just the two of you, you sort of can create your own little world, and you start believing your world, and thinking it's all that's real. If I were to believe everything that Mitch has said, which I sometimes think I do actually believe, I'd probably lie down and never get back up again."

"What are some things he has said to you that you don't know whether to believe or not?"

"Well, there was one time when I walked in on him after just pouring himself some gin. The bottle was on the shelf behind him, the glass was in his hand. I outright asked him, 'Are you drinking again?' He said no. I said, 'Is that gin right there behind you?' He said yes. I asked him again if he were drinking and he said no. Okay, so that's one where I realized he was lying to me, not a good example.

"Umm, a few years ago, I was asked to do take a weekend assignment in DC, and I was so excited and couldn't wait to tell somebody. But when I told Mitch, he just said, 'Huh, I didn't think you were flying-out worthy' and walked away. Like, he was surprised that my boss thought I was good enough to handle that kind of responsibility or to do it well. And I just took that in and figured that was true about me. I ended up telling my boss I couldn't go."

"Do you think you do this often? Take in what Mitch says as the truth of who you really are?"

"I think I do it even more than I realize. He's called me a lying moron, told me that I'm full of bullshit. Early on, I started adding the word *idiot* in my head to the end of his sentences. He would talk to me with such disgust, like he couldn't believe he had married someone

EIGHTEEN

so stupid, that when he would be angry with me, it felt like he was calling me an idiot in his head. Then there were the littler things, things he didn't say. He'd rearrange the dishwasher after I had just done it. He'd change the positioning of the letters in the mailbox so they were "better." He'd sigh when I parked the car not well enough in the garage, roll his eyes, and sometimes re-park it. In one of my job evaluations several years ago, my boss told me that I made decisions quickly, as if I'm scared, and then I would almost always second-guess myself. With how much of an idiot I must be, I'm frankly surprised I kept a job, and have friends, and can parent with any equanimity at all."

"Jules, you're not an idiot. You are not crazy. You are not a liar. You are an honorable woman. I can tell that you love God. I can tell that you love your children. I can tell that you are striving to be emotionally aware. I can tell that your desire is to be as healthy as you can be. *Idiot* and *moron* are awful words and they do not depict who you are. That is not who God says you are."

Dr. Grant got up from his chair and walked over to the bookshelf. He pulled a book out, looked in the table of contents and flipped it open. He handed the book to me, and I saw a pie chart. The title at the top said *the wheel of power and abuse*. In each of the little pie pieces were words like *spiritual abuse, emotional abuse, economic abuse, sexual abuse, physical abuse, the misuse of male privilege*. I scanned it and looked up at him, confused. *Why had he given this to me?*

He said, "I'm going to read each one out loud to you. I want you to just mark with a pencil any of the descriptions that sound like you and Mitch."

"Dr. Grant, I appreciate this, but I'm not abused. Abused women aren't college educated, middle class Christians. Abused women are the stuff of Lifetime TV movies."

"Just listen, keep an open mind. Maybe nothing will ring true. Just humor me, okay?"

He read through each little pie slice, each description, about fourteen in all. And when he was finished, tears were running down my face.

"Did you mark any?" he asked, already knowing the answer.

I nodded.

"How many?"

"Most of them …"

He waited a moment. "Jules, you had no idea, did you?"

"That I'm in an abusive relationship? No," I whispered. "I took psychology classes in college. I thought abuse was physical, like a black eye, or sexual, like rape, or verbal, like being yelled at a lot. And though Mitch yells, I do too, so I just figured …"

"You just figured that your relationship was hard but everyone's marriage is hard, right?"

"What do I do with this? Really, how do I get through this? Listen, I know how counseling works. I really do. You listen. You ask questions. You ask more questions when I ask you what to do. But I really need actual, practical advice. How do I take care of myself? How do I treat Mitch? How do I take care of my kids? What do I do now?"

"You're not going to like my answer."

"Answer me anyway."

"You rest. You pray. You surround yourself with people you trust. You keep going for bike rides to the park. You make your kids dinner. You try to show kindness in the face of anger. You remove yourself when necessary. You do the work. And then you wait and see."

"Wait and see?"

"Nothing like this changes overnight. Mitch may not even realize that what he's doing is wrong. Or if he does, that could be why he drinks, to cover up the guilt and shame. My point is there is no easy fix. But I can help you work through this and figure out what to do."

"Next week then?" I asked, as I stood up, our time already done for the day.

I walked to my car, the sun brighter than I remember it being when I walked in. I breathed in deeply. Everything is different now. Not one thing in my life is the same.

NINETEEN

*T*HERE WERE TWO VOICEMAILS ON my cell when I got out of the appointment. The first was from Brandon. He wanted to invite Mitch and me over for dinner, as soon as possible (read: before Mitch is taken away in handcuffs). That invitation will go over real well, I'm sure. It's going to be a no, I don't even need to ask. But, I'll ask anyway. I'll see what Mitch says. Just hearing Brandon's voice, though, gave me hope. Coupled with that intense session with Dr. Grant, I was catching glimpses of what other people claimed when they said they knew they weren't alone in something. I was finally beginning to feel not alone. What a concept. I would go have dinner with Brandon and Celia, even if Mitch wouldn't.

The second voicemail was from Greg. He was looking for Mitch, and he asked me to call him right away. I didn't want to. I didn't think it was a good idea for me to be talking to him right now, being Miss Vulnerability at this moment. He'll find Mitch; he'll forget he even asked me to call him.

When I got home, Lauren and Macey were sitting on the front porch swing. I love that my daughter has Lauren to confide in. I realized a long time ago that I can't be everything my kids need, and I trust Lauren with my life. Lauren had her arm around Macey's shoulder, Macey's head resting on Lauren's. Lauren gave me a small smile as I walked up the stairs. "Look at my sweet girls. May I join you?"

NINETEEN

Macey nodded, I sat down next to her. "How was counseling?" she asked.

"Good. Hard. Dad didn't come, which was weird, but I'm sure he just needs to be alone right now." I reached for her hand, studied her face.

"You two been talking about anything you want to share? No pressure," I laughed.

"No, we're good, Mom. Lauren was just listening."

"Want to stay for dinner?" I asked my oldest friend. "I have no idea what I'm making yet, but we'd love the company."

"I'd like that, thanks," said Lauren.

"I'm going to take a quick shower before dinner," Macey gave Lauren a side hug, leaving us two friends alone.

"How's my girl doing?" I asked her. "Like, really?"

"She's going to be okay. But right now she's just really sad. She's confused. She's angry. And even though the facts are out there, she doesn't want to believe that her dad is capable of what he did. She's just really hurting right now."

"Yeah, I bet. I'm all those things, and I'm in my forties, it must be doubly hard for her to wrap her head around all this. I mean, really, it's just crazy. This is not the average thing that the average family goes through. I wonder if she'd talk with Dr. Grant … that might help, and he's really great."

"How did your session go?" Lauren asked.

"Oh my word. It was kinda crazy. Ummm, he basically said I'm in an abusive relationship. That Mitch, you know, abuses me. Like a lot." I said this, shaking my head, still in disbelief. "Crazy, right?"

I looked at Lauren. "Not all that crazy," she said.

"What do you mean?"

"I mean, I could have told you that, like, before you even got married. I thought you knew, just that you didn't want to deal with it or something."

"Huh. It's that obvious? People must think I'm an absolute fool! What kind of woman lets someone treat her like this, let alone for over twenty years?"

"No, Sweetheart. You're not a fool. You're not any of the things Mitch has told you that you are. And it's only obvious to me because I've seen you guys up-close for so many years, and because you share stuff with me. Like, remember the time you told me that you stood in front of the thermostat fanning it and begging Jesus to make the temperature go down before Mitch walked in the door? That's something an abused woman would do, Babe. I'm so sorry. This must be a lot to take in, especially in the middle of all this."

"I'm a little numb. Dr. Grant says I just need to sort of do what's next. I need to get rest, and ride my bike, and talk to my friends, and make dinner for my kids. So, for today, that's what I'm going to do. Tomorrow will have to figure itself out, because I barely have the energy to get through to bedtime."

"Hey, what do you think your mom would say to you right now?"

I chewed on my lip before guessing, "She'd probably tell me that she's sorry for what she didn't teach me along the way about getting through something like this. She'd probably tell me that God is watching me. She'd probably tell me it's all going to turn out okay … and she'd probably tell me to go to a meeting." I laughed. "It's pretty amazing that I feel like I really know her now from reading those letters, that I could actually figure out what she might be thinking."

"That is a total gift, Hon." We sat quietly for a minute. "Shifting gears a bit, and I hate to even bring this up, but, how's Mitch?" Lauren asked.

"I haven't seen him since last night, and when I did, it wasn't pretty. And he hasn't checked in at all. Greg called me looking for him a little while ago, but I'm sure he'll turn up. So, I don't know how Mitch is, but if I had to guess, I'd say not good."

"Hmm … I'm sorry, Honey. Hey, I'll go get dinner ready. Why don't you lie down for a bit?" Lauren asked as she stood up.

"That would be good. Thanks," I said. Lauren went inside.

As I walked up the stairs, I passed a picture of my mother and me when I was a little girl. I wish my mom were here to get me through this. Seeing this picture reminds me of another photograph I used to have of the two of us. It was taken on my sixteenth birthday. It is the

NINETEEN

last picture I have of her and me, about a year before she died. She is sitting in a chair at a long table in a restaurant, and I had come up behind her, and wrapped my arms around her, our faces pressed together. We're both smiling and looking at my dad, who is taking the picture. I miss my mom, and I miss that picture. I could always look at that picture and know that she loved me.

I don't have that picture anymore. My husband stole it from me. It was here when I left for my time away with Lauren, but when I came back, it was gone. In its place was the picture that had been behind it in the frame, a picture of Mitch and me from about ten years before. When I got home and saw that the picture was gone, I immediately called him. It went to voicemail so I left him a message. *"Where is my mother's picture?"* I'm sure I yelled this. I was beside myself. When he didn't respond, I sent him a text: "WHERE IS MY MOTHER'S PICTURE?" Who does something like that? He didn't respond to the text either. When he got home, I asked him again. He just looked at me, smirked, and walked out of the room.

There are moments, as hard as it is to believe, when I think to myself, *Maybe, it really isn't that bad after all. Maybe, I am blowing everything out of proportion. Maybe, I just need to develop a thicker skin.* But then, I remember my mother's picture. I imagine it buried at the bottom of Mitch's closet, or somewhere on his workbench in the garage. Or, worse, at a garbage dump, because he doesn't even have it and got rid of it ages ago.

So, I remember that missing picture, and I remind myself that this man that I am married to is now a sick man. This man knows this is the last picture I have of me and my mom, and this man knows how much I loved her, and he not only stole it from me, he is keeping it from me intentionally to hurt me.

This is now the bar that I look to. This is now my ultimate reminder of over twenty years of abuse, and manipulation, and lies, and control, and downright unkindness. This is my touchstone, the thing that points to his sickness and his depravity, and that nothing has changed in him, except perhaps he is becoming worse and worse of a human being with each day that he holds onto it. He should be ashamed of himself, but he's not. I need to keep reminding me of this, keep pulling this picture back to the forefront of my mind, because I have a feeling it's just going to get harder before it gets better, and it's crucial to remember that what I'm dealing with is insanity.

And if I had to guess, I will never see that picture of my mom and me again. And if I had to guess, there are a lot of things that will never happen again.

TWENTY

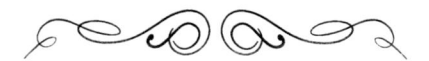

I woke to the sound of Jordan's voice and him knocking on my door. "Mom, wake up. Greg's here. Mom?"

"I'm awake, I'm awake. Is he here to see your dad?"

"No, he says he needs to talk to you," he said. "He seems upset."

Without checking myself in the mirror, I grabbed my robe and headed downstairs. "Morning, Greg. What's up? Is something wrong?"

"Can we talk outside, Jay?" I shot him a look that told him again how much I hated that he called me that, especially in front of Jordan. I don't need my kid wondering why his dad's best friend has a nickname for me.

I followed him out to the porch. "What's up?" I asked again, more impatient this time.

"It's about Mitch. I tried calling you yesterday. I got this text from him, and it has me worried." He handed me his phone, which read, "YOU WERE A GOOD FRIEND."

"Okay? Maybe he's feeling all nostalgic now that he's facing prison time."

"Jay, it says *were*. You *were* a good friend. Past tense. Doesn't that seem weird to you?"

"I guess.... I don't know, Greg. What do you want me to say?"

"When was the last time you saw him?"

TWENTY

"Two nights ago. I think he left sometime yesterday morning, he didn't answer my text, and he didn't come home last night. I know that's kind of odd behavior, even for him, but I'm sure it's all just normal for what he's going through."

"If for nothing else, though, don't you think the police should know since he wasn't supposed to leave the state? I'm not saying that he did, but you just never know. His drinking has been getting worse. Maybe he just took off somewhere."

"How many hours is it before someone is considered missing?"

"I think it's twenty-four, but I'm not sure. I really think you should call the police, Jules. I just don't feel right about all this."

"Alright. Can I use your cell?" I sat down on the swing. He sat next to me, handed me his phone.

I dialed 911. "Hi, this is Jules Millhouse. My husband hasn't been home in over thirty-six hours, and I'm sure he's fine, but he was just convicted of a crime and was told not to leave the state, so I think somebody should be notified just in case. Oh, okay. Sure. Alright, thank you."

"What did they say?"

"I have to go in to the station to file a report. Come with me. Please," I put my hand on Greg's.

"Yeah, of course."

"I just have to get dressed. Wait out here for me, okay?"

I ran into the house and found the kids in the living room, watching TV. "Hey guys, you okay for a little while? I have an errand to run. I should be back in an hour or two, I think."

"We're fine, Mom. Everything okay with Greg?" Macey asked.

"Yeah, he just needs my help with something. Nothing to worry about," I said, mentally crossing my fingers.

I let Greg drive. A numbness was beginning to fall over me. I'd heard other people say that during certain moments of their lives, they felt like they were watching a movie. I was having one of those moments. I had never walked into a police station before this moment. Part of me expected to be interrogated myself. What kind of wife waits thirty-six hours to call when her husband doesn't come home? *An abused one,* would be my silent answer if actually asked.

Greg came around to my side of the car to open the door and held out his hand to help me out. He then placed his hand on my elbow and led me inside. Was he secretly relishing being my rescuing knight in the middle of this crisis? I had to push those thoughts aside for the moment as the officer behind the counter asked what I needed.

"I called earlier. My husband hasn't been home for a day-and-a-half. I was told to come in to file a report."

"Alright. I'm going to need you to fill this out, and then bring it back up when you're finished."

I sat down with a clipboard and with shaking hands, I filled in everything I remembered. Name, birthdate, social security number. I had no idea what Mitch's drivers' license number was. *Would a better wife know that?* I only remembered the first few letters and numbers of his license plate. Hopefully they can look that up easily enough. Make and model of car. Year, color. Got it.

I handed the form back in and was called a few minutes later to talk with the sergeant.

"Ma'am, have a seat. I pulled your husband's file. He's got several DUI's on his record. Did you know about those?"

"No, I didn't."

"Where was the last place you saw him?"

"At home, two nights ago."

"What was he doing? Did you two have a conversation?"

"He was in the basement alone, drinking. He didn't even see me. So, no, we didn't talk right then. But that was the day of his sentencing, so he was pretty upset."

"What was the last thing you remember him saying to you? Was there anything odd about it?"

"He told me somewhat jokingly that I didn't have to 'wait for him' when he goes to prison. It was a brief conversation. Nothing that I thought was out of the ordinary, really. However, he did send a text to his best friend. He came with me. It said something like 'you were

TWENTY

a good friend.' It's maybe a little cryptic that he said 'were' instead of 'are.' What do you think?"

The officer got up and walked over to Greg. I couldn't hear what they were saying, but I saw Greg pull out his phone and show the officer the text. He led Greg back to his desk, and they both sat down.

"It looks like he sent that yesterday morning. So, as far as we know, he was still alive about twenty-four hours ago."

"What? He was *still alive*? What are you talking about?" My words came out loud and sharp.

Greg reached for my hand. "He thinks that Mitch might've done something to hurt himself."

The officer looked at me, "Mrs. Millhouse, in this situation, with how long he's been gone, him not answering your texts, his text to Mr. Grafton, the DUI's, and him just finding out about his sentencing, things don't look good, I have to be honest. We're going to put an APB out on your husband. There's really nothing else you can do right now, just make sure I've got your contact information, and we'll be in touch if anything comes up. And please, let us know if you hear from him."

I sat in the chair, my legs unable to move. Greg took my hand again, looked at me with a head nod. I stood up and we walked out. I don't remember the drive home.

After Greg dropped me off, I walked into the house to find Macey and Jordan waiting for me, waiting for answers. "We know something's wrong, Mom," said Macey. "Please just tell us what's going on."

I poured myself a glass of water, trying to figure out how to say this. "Okay, so here's the thing. No one has seen your dad since the other night, and Greg and I are concerned that he may have tried to take off since he found out he's guilty and up for prison time. We don't know where he is, and so we just went to the police station to file a report. They are going to start searching for him. I'm sure he's okay, though, and just got scared." I looked at my children. *Children.* They are still just children. How much more are they supposed to take on?

"Wait, so, you have no idea where Dad is, and you don't really know for sure if he's okay?" Jordan.

"Technically, yes. But I just …"

"How can you not know? How can you just sit here and wait? How could he be so stupid to run away? Like that's going to make things better when he gets back? He's just made everything harder. For him. For us … He always just thinks of himself."

"Jor, I know. I know this is crazy and hard and confusing. It doesn't make any sense. But I'm guessing that your dad is scared. I would be too, wouldn't you? I'm not saying running away was a good idea. In fact, it was foolish. But getting mad at Dad right now isn't going to do any of us any good. We just really need to pray that he's found soon, so we can move on with trying to figure all this out." I took his face in my hands and made him look me in the eyes. "It's going to be okay. Do you hear me?"

He shook himself out of my grip. "You don't know that, Mom." He walked out. He was right, I didn't know that.

Macey, "What are we going to do? We should go looking for him."

"Hon, I really think we should stay home, in case he calls or comes back, and just let the police do their job. We wouldn't know where to look anyway."

There was a knock on the kitchen door as my dad walked in. "Macey called me. She said something seemed wrong when you left here with Greg. What's going on?"

At this, Macey said, "If you're not going to look, I will," grabbing the car keys and heading out the door faster than I could stop her.

"Macey, wait …" My shoulders slumped.

"Look for what? What's all that about?" my father said.

"Mitch is missing. He's *missing*, Dad." He walked over to me and held me, for the first time in years. And I let him. And I cried. "What am I going to do? I don't know what to do."

"You're not going to do anything. They'll find him. He couldn't have gotten too far." His arm was still around me. "Why don't you go freshen up? I'll make you some tea, and then I'll go track down your kids and bring them back home."

TWENTY

"Thank you, Dad. I'm not sure I could do this on my own right now."

"Well, you don't have to." The words were gruff, but full, as they tumbled from his mouth.

───※───

After taking a quick shower, I laid down on my bed. The whirring of the ceiling fan lulled me to sleep as one thought kept marching across my brain like a parade. *Mitch is missing. Mitch is missing. Jesus, Mitch is missing.* I dreamt of overturned cars and police sirens, of screams and bridges, of crying, of little white crosses, of my kids in black.

A text came through, shaking me back to reality. It was Lauren, "I've tried calling you. COME TO THE PARK NOW."

"Coming," I texted back. I ran downstairs and realized I didn't have a car. Mitch had his car, Macey had mine. I jumped on my bike and rode as fast as I could to the park, my breathing labored. A police car passed me, sirens on, heading in the same direction.

I'm sure it's a coincidence. I'm sure it's nothing. Jesus, where is Mitch? Where is Jordan? Where is Macey? Where is my dad? Where is everybody? I'm alone. I'm alone. I can't do this alone.

You're not alone.

I jumped off my bike, letting it fall to the ground next to Lauren's car in the parking lot. I saw Lauren across the field at the edge of the woods, where the trail starts up along the ravine. As I ran closer, I could see she was holding someone. Macey. *Why is she holding Macey? Why are the police here? The police shouldn't be here.*

Macey looked up and ran to me, falling into my arms. "It's Daddy! I found Daddy." She was shaking, wet, sobbing. I looked at Lauren, begging her with my eyes to tell me what Macey was talking about. Lauren nodded toward the river. I handed Macey back off to Lauren and walked to the edge. The front half of Mitch's car was submerged just past the back seat, with the trunk pointing towards the sky.

"Ma'am, you need to step back. This is a police investigation," the officer said.

"That's my husband's car," I said. I hunched down to get a better look. I could see through the rear windshield. I spotted the watch

I gave him on the hand that was gripping the steering wheel. "And that's my ... that's my husband," I said, falling back to the ground. *You're not alone*, I heard as I slipped away.

※

I opened my eyes, Lauren standing over me. "Sit up slowly, Honey," she said. The first thing I saw was Mitch's car, ten feet away. There was a beeping sound as a tow truck was backing up into place, preparing to pull the car, and Mitch, out of the ravine. "Oh God ... no."

Lauren said, "Jules, you need to be strong right now for the kids. Macey is talking to the police, giving her statement. You need to be with her. I got a hold of your dad, and he found Jordan. They're waiting at the house for you. You can freak out later."

She was right. I stood up. There was no time for grieving or losing it. I had to be the strong one. I walked over to Macey and the officer. "I don't know why I came to the park. I just had this feeling," she told him.

"Did your father tell you where he was going? Did he contact you after he left?"

"No, I just came here. I just ..." She started to cry again.

I put my arm around her. "Officer, if you have any other questions for her, they're going to have to wait. I need to get her home."

Lauren threw my bike in her trunk and got Macey situated. I watched the tow truck pulling my husband's casket out of the water. *How does something like this happen? Something's not right. I know he was desperate, but I can't imagine he would kill himself.*

Nothing about this is right.

※

I had Lauren take Macey in through the front door and up to my room. I went in through the kitchen and asked my dad and Jordan to come with me into the living room. *I don't have the words for this, Jesus. You have to give me the words.*

I sat on the coffee table directly in front of Jordan. I placed my hand on his knee. I looked straight at him even though he wouldn't

TWENTY

hold my gaze. "Jordan." He looked up. "Daddy was found. His car was in the ravine, over at the park. He was in it. He wasn't alive when they found him." My dad gasped and got up quickly, knocking into the table with his knee as he left the room.

Jordan didn't say anything.

"Jordan? Do you understand what I'm saying about Dad?"

"Dad's dead. I get it."

"Yes. Daddy's gone."

"Stop calling him Daddy."

"Okay, I'm sorry."

"So, he killed himself?" He was talking as if we were discussing a TV show or something.

"The police are trying to figure some things out, Honey. We don't know yet all that happened."

"Did you see his body?"

"Yes."

"What did it look like?"

"I didn't get a good look; he was still in the car, and the car was still in the water. A tow truck was just pulling the car out as we were leaving."

"So, he got out of going to jail, huh?"

"Okay, Jordan, I don't like your tone here. No matter what happened or what he did or did not do, he was still your father. He loved you."

"He loved me? Yeah, right."

"Oh Babe, he did. I know things have been hard lately, the past few years. I know he didn't always show it anymore. But he did. He adored you. I need you to never forget that."

A tear rolled down his cheek but he brushed it away as swiftly as it appeared. I moved to the couch next to him. I pulled my little boy, my young man, close to me and wrapped both arms around him. *Jesus, help him to believe that his dad really loved him. Please. He needs to believe this now.*

After breaking the news to Jordan and my father, I got M
in my bed. She fell asleep almost instantly, and I asked L
with her. Jordan sat on the couch, holding the remote, the television off. My father was in the kitchen making us soup. *Since when did he learn how to make soup?*

The doorbell rang. Two police officers and Greg arrived at the same time: Greg for comfort, the police for more questions. We settled in the formal living room.

After the initial questioning, one of the officers said, "Mrs. Millhouse, your husband's blood alcohol level was three times the legal limit. That, coupled with the tire tracks indicating the simultaneous acceleration and braking, leads us to believe that he didn't mean to drive into the ravine. As of now, we're deeming this case an accidental suicide. I hope that puts some of your concerns to rest."

"Umm, okay ... thank you. Greg, can you show them out, assuming we're done for right now?"

"Sure," he said, walking them to the front door.

I sat on the couch, a pillow in my lap, protecting me from my life, and that conversation, and my widowhood.

Greg came back in and sat next to me. I leaned against his shoulder. I looked up at him, "This is all so crazy. What do I do now?" He moved toward me and kissed me. I kissed him back for just a moment, then pulled away. "Greg! *Really?* My husband just died. Today! I need your support, but I can't do *this* right now! You have to go."

"Jay, I'm sorry. That was wrong."

"Just go, Greg. We're fine ... it's okay ... but I need you to go."

I didn't remember falling asleep, but I woke up in the middle of the night on the couch. I forgot where I was and why I wasn't in my bed. For about six seconds. Then it hit me. Mitch was dead. I had prayed for this. I had asked God to take my husband away, so I wouldn't have to bear being married to him anymore. "I killed my husband," I whispered to the dark.

TWENTY-ONE

*J*MOVED THROUGH THE HOUSE LIKE a ghost, quiet and floating. Jordan was asleep on the living room couch, my father in the recliner. I looked out the window to see Lauren's car, so she must have been upstairs with Macey.

I let myself out the kitchen door and made my way around to the front of the house. The stars were bright. I could see my breath. It was the kind of silence that usually scares me, but I let it wrap around me. Nothing would scare me anymore. My husband was gone. The abuse was now over. The daily obsession with his addiction could cease. My constant begging for affection from that man could finally stop. The fighting would be behind me.

And, on the other side of things, I will be alone. I will parent by myself, and my children will no longer have a father. And, I hate funerals. What will I talk about or think about if I can't talk and think about all of my problems with Mitch? He gave me something to do. I will have nothing to do. I will have nothing to think about.

I could use a drink. Except that I don't drink.

Okay, some questions, for God, for the night sky, for whomever: How do I not be married anymore? How do I get my kids through this? Mitch is dead. How will I get through this? How do I forgive Mitch for driving himself into the river? He's dead. How do I accept God's forgiveness for asking that he kill off my husband? How do I

TWENTY-ONE

not lose my mind? (Is it too late for that one?) How will I be alone? I haven't been alone in twenty-five years. No, that's not true. I've already been alone for ages.

Jesus, this one is specifically for you. Where are you? And one more, Will you help me? And another one, who am I now?

He's dead.

DAYS LATER

*T*HE SANCTUARY FEELS DIFFERENT. THE light is hurting my eyes and it's colder. I never sit in the first row. I don't look good in black. This dress is totally inappropriate. Why didn't anyone stop me from wearing this thing? And, why did I agree to have everyone over at the house after this? How am I going to pull that off?

I'm not supposed to be glad that he's dead. Okay, I guess *glad* isn't the right word. Relieved maybe?

I should probably be listening to the eulogy. *Jordan, stop messing with your tie*, I glare at my son. I can't believe he wore sneakers. And Macey, well, she's crying enough for the both of us.

I want this day to be over.

No, I'm not just relieved. I *am* glad. I'm glad my husband is dead.

TWO YEARS FROM NOW

IT'S TAKEN ME THIS ENTIRE year to slowly move from room to room through our home, weeding out all of Mitch's belongings. I saved the basement for last, as it was always my least favorite room in the house during our marriage. The darkness there always seemed to hang a heavy veil over our every conversation. We had more fights down there. He lied to me more down there. He hid so much from me down there. But I knew I had to get to it eventually, so the anniversary of his death seemed morose, and yet oddly fitting. I would clear the entire place out by the end of the day, throwing out most of what I would find. He didn't have mementos. It was mostly junk: old papers that weren't needed anymore, boxes for electronics we no longer owned, mason jars filled with paper clips, screws, and pennies.

I'm doing this room on my own. Though Macey is back from college, she's with friends for the day, and Jordan's at camp. This year has been healing and crazy and hard on both of them, so very hard. Macey, gratefully, was able to start seeing a counselor at school, and she texts me a couple times a day. She may have her ups and downs, but at least I'll always know how she's feeling. And Jordan is still quiet, still keeps to himself. But with it just being the two of us, he is opening up a bit more here and there. Brandon has really stepped in with him, taking him out for breakfast a couple times a month. They are these gorgeous kids who love life, love me and love God. I can finally say that I fully believe they're going to both be okay.

As for me, I'm less of a mess than I was during our marriage. Some days, not much less. There was so much to undo, more than I had realized. The damage had gone into my soul. But I'm finally catching glimpses of hope, of healing, even, and, I can't believe I'm saying this, of joy. I don't miss him, though. We had stopped being friends so long ago. Or maybe we never really were. I never quite felt one with him.

After hours of going through one box after another, and not surprisingly coming across liquor store receipts and brown bags with empty bottles inside, something caught my eye. I pushed some papers aside, bank statements from a decade ago, and saw the list. You know the list. The list of what I had wanted in a marriage, the list Mitch claimed to not remember asking for, the one he had asked for when he had been drunk, apparently. The one he told me he wouldn't be reading, because he never read anything I wrote. The one I had found crumpled up a few months before he died. That list.

This time though it was flattened, as if someone had tried to smooth out every crease. And written across the top of list, in black marker, all caps, "I'M SORRY." I dropped to the floor. He was sorry.

Today is the first truly beautiful day of summer. *He was sorry.* I'm finally learning to breathe again. *He was sorry.* I'm finally learning who I am. *He was sorry.* I'm finally feeling the peace that God has always meant for me to feel. *Sorry.*

Who am I, Jesus?

For a year I have berated myself for not trying hard enough to save our marriage, to save Mitch from himself. For a year I have beat myself up for not doing enough when in reality I did every single thing I knew how to do. For a year I have scolded myself for not missing him.

I don't miss us. But I miss who he was supposed to be. Our story wasn't supposed to end like it did or when it did. I can see that now.

"It's been a hard year, Mitch," I sat down next to his gravestone. "I have some things I need to say to you."

I closed my eyes. I sat up straight. I pulled the sheet of paper out of my purse.

I cleared my throat. "Did you ever know that I really did love you once? Did you know that I dragged around so much guilt for letting you down, for not being the wife that you wanted and probably needed, that I still do? Did you ever know that I will always be grateful to you for Macey and Jordan? Did you ever know that there really were some things about you that I not only liked, but I loved? Did you ever know that I missed the man you were, the man you were supposed to be, the way you made me laugh?

"I'm guessing not. I stopped telling you these things a long time ago. I couldn't bear to say them to you, to say them out loud, because I couldn't bear to admit them to myself. I didn't want to need you or love you or even like you anymore. It made it easier, and I needed something in my life, something in our marriage, to be easier.

"If I let myself feel things for you, to keep loving you with the intensity that I did at the beginning, the pain of watching you kill yourself, and slowly leave us every day, would have driven me to an insanity of sorts. At least, a different kind of insanity than I already was living in. Because, how do you stand by and watch someone you deeply love hurt himself over and over again, every single day? How do you not step in? How do you not do everything you can to stop them?

"But what you had, this drinking disease, is a different beast, Mitch. There was no stopping it. It's the only ailment I know of where the person it's happening to is also the one who made it happen, and the only one who can make it stop. Doctors couldn't make you stop. Pastors couldn't make you stop. Sons and daughters couldn't make you stop. God couldn't make you stop (or at least, he *wouldn't* because of free will and all).

But, perhaps most especially, your wife couldn't make you stop.

"I tried everything I knew. Did you ever know that? Did you know that intermingled with the prayers of an out, I prayed for *you*? I prayed you'd get caught. I prayed you'd get DUIs. I prayed that someone at work would notice and say something. I prayed someone from church would notice and do something. I prayed you'd wake up one day and realize that you were throwing your life away, one bottle, one sip at a time. And I begged you, Mitch. This I know you know. I cried, I yelled, I screamed, I threatened, I made up rules, I gave you ultimatums. But it didn't matter. Not one thing I ever did helped, because only you could stop. And even then, I'm not sure you could.

"Why did this have to happen to you, to us? Why did this have to come into our lives and set up shop, and move in and become part of our family, and break us apart one day at a time? Why weren't you strong enough in the beginning to put the brakes on? Why wasn't I strong enough to walk away before we both did so much untold damage to each other?

"I'm so sorry, Mitch. I'm so, so sorry for my part in our destruction, in your downfall. I did love you once. I really, really did. Did you ever know?" I shifted, stared at the stone, and brushed away some dead leaves.

"I forgive you, Mitch. Really. For all of it. For over twenty years of lies and pain and abuse. But here's what you need to know. My forgiving you does not mean that any of the things that you did were okay. My forgiving you does not mean that I will forget. In fact, I keep asking God to lessen the memories so that my heart doesn't hurt all the time when I think about you, but I believe it's important that we remember when we've been hurt, so that we can protect ourselves from it in the future.

"I am saying that I forgive you, despite the fact that you more than likely always just thought I was being overdramatic. I am saying that I forgive you, despite the fact that you did next to nothing to ever try to earn my trust back, or my love. In other words, Mitch, I am forgiving you in spite of you. I am forgiving you, not because of anything that you did, but solely because of what Jesus has done for me. And I am finally ready to forgive you once and for all because I need to be free."

Tears rolled down my cheeks. I reached into my purse and pulled out another piece of paper, The List. On top of my wishes for our marriage, across Mitch's *I'M SORRY*, I had written *FORGIVEN*.

"And Mitch, I'm sorry. I wasn't a good wife. I didn't know how to love you. I demanded so much from you, too much. I know you can't forgive me, but I just needed you to know this. I am so sorry."

I placed the letter I just read and the marriage list into an envelope, and tucked it between one of the plants and the gravestone. I gathered my things, stood up, and walked back to the car. Some burdens are meant to be laid down.

Who am I, Jesus?

Forgiven. Free. Loved. Healing.

Sometimes a world split open can be put back together, after all, one small piece at a time.

Dear Macey and Jordan,

My mom wrote me letters as I was growing up, and they have become such a treasure to me. So, I wanted to share some of my thoughts with you too.

Our early life together, the four of us, has been difficult. Though there have been secrets along the way, this is not one of them, mainly because there was no denying it.

Let me first say, I am so sorry for my part in it, for the part I played in keeping secrets. I'm sorry for taking so long to get help for myself, and offer true help to each of you. I'm sorry for the way I spoke to your father, in and out of your presence. I'm sorry for the ways that our difficulties made me more self-absorbed and less available to each of you emotionally as you grew up. I'd so like to fall back on the cliché that I was doing the best I could, but I'm not sure that's the case. I was hurting, and because of that I was not fully there for you two, and I am so sorry.

My hope and prayer for both of you is that you each follow after what God wants for your lives, that you treat each other kindly as adults. I pray that you find a life partner who will support you and understand you, who you will support and seek to understand. And, if you ever find yourself sinking in any way, that you'll turn to Jesus and turn for help. Waves will come and there will be situations in life that will feel overwhelming, but he can and will get you through anything. But here's the key ... only if you let him. So please, sweet children, let him.

    I love you with all of my heart,

                                                                                      Mom

IF YOU ARE IN A HURTING MARRIAGE, HERE ARE A FEW THINGS YOU CAN DO

Pray. Pray for yourself, pray for your spouse, pray for healing.
Read Scripture. Immerse yourself in God's word. Get into a Bible study.
Read other resources.
> *Surviving in a Difficult Christian Marriage* by Elisabeth Klein
> *The Emotionally Destructive Marriage* by Leslie Vernick
> *The Power of a Praying Wife* by Stormie Omartian
> *The Verbally Abusive Relationship* by Patricia Evans
> *How to Act Right When Your Spouse Acts Wrong* by Leslie Vernick
> *Boundaries in Marriage* by Cloud & Townsend
> *Thriving Despite a Difficult Marriage* by Michael Misja
> *Foolproofing Your Life* by Jan Silvious
> *Love Isn't Supposed to Hurt* by Christi Paul
> *Why Does He Do That* by Lundy Bancroft
> *Smart Women Know When to Say No* by Dr. Kevin Leman
> *Shattered Vows: Hope and Healing for Women Who Have Been Sexually Betrayed* by Debra Laaser

IF YOU ARE IN A HURTING MARRIAGE, HERE ARE A FEW THINGS YOU CAN DO

Every Heart Restored by Steve Arterburn
Holding On to Heaven While Your Marriage Goes Through Hell by Connie Neal
Necessary Endings by Henry Cloud
Divorce and Remarriage in the Church by David Instone-Brewer
Domestic abuse Bible studies

Surround yourself with wise counsel.

Make sure your friends are women who love Christ, who hold you accountable and pray for you.

Get into a recovery group. If your spouse has an addiction, try Celebrate Recovery or Al-Anon.

Go to counseling. Find a counselor who bases their treatment on the Word of God.

Talk to your church leadership. Find someone whom you trust, and ask them for help until you receive it.

However, if you or your children are being physically hurt, you must remove yourself from the situation and get help. Not sure if you are being emotionally abused? Determine where you stand in the Wheel Power and Control: http://tinyurl.com/msfx7cg

To find a local Al-Anon group: http://www.al-anon.alateen.org/

To find a local Celebrate Recovery group: http://www.celebraterecovery.com/

To find a local DivorceCare group: http://www.divorcecare.org/

To find a local Christian counselor: http://www.biblicalcounseling.com/counselors

To create a safety plan: http://www.domesticviolence.org/personalized-safety-plan/

Join me in one of my private Facebook groups, *A Place for Us*, specifically for Christian women in hurting marriages or going through difficult divorces. Email me at elisabeth@elisabethklein.com for more information. You will find comfort and encouragement, and you'll know you're not alone.

REFERENCES

1. Unger, Justin/Faircloth, Scott. "I Will Go Before." Recorded by Justin Unger on *Disengage*. Heights Music Group, 2008. MP3
2. Al-Anon Family Group Headquarters. "How Al-Anon Works for Families." 2008.

CONTACT INFORMATION

REDEMPTION PRESS

To order additional copies of this book, please
visit www.redemption-press.com.
Also available on Amazon.com and BarnesandNoble.com
or by calling toll free 1 (844) 2REDEEM (273-3336).

CPSIA information can be obtained at www.ICGtesting.com
Printed in the USA
LVOW11s0346180914

404575LV00003B/61/P

9 781632 326614